Rain Town

Rain Town

Andy Donaldson

Matador
9 Priory Business Park,
Wistow Road, Kibworth Beauchamp,
Leicestershire, LE8 0RX
Tel: 0116 279 2299
Email: books@troubador.co.uk
Web: www.troubador.co.uk/matador
Twitter: @matadorbooks

ISBN 978 1789016 833

British Library Cataloguing in Publication Data.
A catalogue record for this book is available from the British Library.

Printed and bound by CPI Group (UK) Ltd, Croydon, CR0 4YY
Typeset in 12pt Bembo by Troubador Publishing Ltd, Leicester, UK

Matador is an imprint of Troubador Publishing Ltd

For Mark and Mia

A huge, heartfelt thank you to all those who have advised and supported me in the making of Rain Town. Special thanks to Caroline, David and Anne for your encouragement and all the staff at Troubador for bringing it to life.

Chapter One

HE COULDN'T HAVE been more than fifteen years old. The hoodie around his shoulders and head kept his face and identity secret from the world. His pulse raced in his neck and his fingers fumbled in his pockets as he waited for the opportunity to present itself. Every so often he would take a quick, furtive glance towards the shop owner, who was busy watching the football on the small television fastened to the wall above his counter. His young heart pumped away. The shop owner reacted to something that happened in the football match; his arms leapt into the air in exasperation. And in that moment, the hooded youth, quick as a flash, grabbed several chocolate bars from the shelf and wrestled them away inside his hoodie. Over the next minute, he wandered casually around the small shop with the owner apparently blissfully unaware of the theft taking place right under his nose. As he ranted and raved at the television, pockets were being filled with all manner of treasure. Crisps, chocolate, sweets and cans of pop were all being stealthily and illegally harvested. Another few seconds and the boy would be out of the fluorescent light of the shop and into the darkness, mission accomplished.

The shop door closed behind him. With a big grin on his face and his arms clasped around the stolen paraphernalia in his hoodie and pockets, he bounded down the street away from the scene of the crime and into the cover of the welcoming blackness of the night.

Suddenly, he was snapped out of his focus by the screech of a cat down the alleyway across the road. There was an additional noise; a commotion. There were some bumps and thuds and a rustling in the air that suggested that someone else was also present. The young boy stopped. The only sound that he could now hear was the pulse of his heartbeat throbbing in his ears.

"Is there anyone there?" he tentatively enquired of the shadows.

There was no response. *Must have been a cat*, he thought. His pulse calmed and he wiped the sweat from his brow. The young thief turned away from the alley and the road and once more urged his feet to move on.

"What are you doing, little boy?" commanded a booming voice from the alleyway.

The shock caused him to drop a few packets of sweets and crisps onto the pavement at his feet.

"Who's… who is… it?" said the youth. His voice was frightened and timid.

"I asked you a question. What are you doing, naughty boy?"

"Nothing," he replied. "I've just been shopping."

The voice in the alleyway became a visible shadow in the half-light. "So you are proficient at lying as well as stealing. From where I was, it looked remarkably like you took those items without paying for them," the shadow barked.

"I'm only borrowing them," said the boy. "I'll give them back later."

"You and I both know that isn't true. The truth is, little boy, that it is way past your bedtime and you shouldn't be out at this time of night. Something nasty could happen to you," warned the mysterious figure as he stepped a little further into view.

That sounded like a threat. The youngster was shaking a little now, as if the temperature had dropped a few degrees. The man in the alley seemed big; six foot plus, he mused. Half out of curiosity and half out of terror, his eyes dared to focus in on the adult opposite. The dim light failed to reveal what he probably wasn't that keen to see anyway. The man seemed to have muscles creeping out from his chest and some sort of shiny dark cloak on, because something fluttered in the breeze down by the sides of his legs. Was he wearing a mask? Were those boots that had scraped along the pavement?

"Who are you, Mister? What do you want?"

A man in a jet-black cloak stepped forward into the glare of the street light. He had a strange, dark blue mask covering his face, a thick belt around his waist, and a pair of boots on his feet.

"Do you know who I am now?" asked the masked man.

The thief thought for a moment, screwing his eyes up as he looked the man up and down. "Not really, no."

The caped crusader tutted disappointedly and pointed his finger at his mask, cape and boots, urging recognition from his puzzled observer. "Isn't it obvious?"

"Are you Batman?" the boy suggested.

The masked man looked despondent. He placed his fists at the sides of his belt and his black cloak wafted behind him.

"I'm the Raven!" he announced in a strong, triumphant voice.

The youngster was unimpressed and looked somewhat puzzled. "I've never heard of him."

At this point, the young thief sped off down the street, awkwardly spilling bars of chocolate and bags of sweets as the contents of his hoodie were abandoned in the pursuit of a quick getaway. Cans of fizzy drink tumbled out, ricocheting off the road like shell cartridges ejected from a gun. The masked man reacted quickly too; his boots scraping the tarmac as his body heaved into action with the cape on his back drifting horizontally in the resulting draught. The race was now on, with the street lights illuminating the chase down the dimly lit roads of Shigbeth town. At first the youth feared being caught as he heard his pursuer's boots pounding the ground immediately behind him. He frantically ran harder as he strained to escape capture. His heart pumped ferociously in his ribcage and his lungs cranked in and out like bellows.

About a minute later, however, it started to dawn on him that he was now the only one running, and all that he could hear was the slapping of the soles of his shoes on the pavement beneath him. He slowed down and came to a rest. Breathing heavily and pulling his hood down, he glanced back. There was nobody there. The amateur superhero had gone. As he recovered, he retraced his steps a little back down the road, just to make sure. Soon, he heard blowing and sharp gasps for air coming from behind a garden wall. There he was, the masked vigilante, leant against the bricks, huffing and puffing, and crouched over in exhaustion, his oversized stomach hanging over the edge of his belt. The youth edged a bit closer, more confident in his ability to escape if required from his unfit adversary.

"I recognise you now, Mister," he chirped cockily. "You're not Batman. You're Fatman."

The defeated apparent superhero didn't respond. He just stared back, red cheeks under his mask, unable to find the breath to speak.

The thief sniffed the air and cracked a wide grin. His shoes scratched the ground as he twisted on his feet and took off down the street, celebrating his freedom.

Chapter Two

IT TOOK ABOUT five minutes or so for 'the Raven' to recover. His legs hurt. His back hurt. His pride hurt. There were a few chocolate bars strewn across the pavement that the young thief had dropped. He picked one of them up and slipped it into his pocket in case he got peckish on the way home. Slowly, he scuttled away, back into the shadows from where he came with a limp and a grimace. The mask had now been taken off and his face revealed bright red cheeks and a layer of sweat. The cloak had been removed too, and underneath was a middle-aged, slightly overweight, puffed-out man finding his way back home in his dark green wellington boots at midnight. He took the backstreets home, using the alleyways and avoiding the attention of street lights and car headlights. Nobody saw him as he turned into Bedlam Road and tiptoed up the drive of Number 71. There was a small gap between the fence and the garage, which he only just about squeezed his stomach through, and from then on he crept around the back of the garage to the back door, which he had purposely left unlocked. The door was closed quietly behind him and the key was turned in the lock with a satisfying metallic crunch. Sidney Rain was home.

Next to the back door was a small shower room, into which he sneaked. The boots were peeled off along with the rest of his clothes and he placed them all, including the mask, belt and cape, in a large bag which he wedged in the cupboard under the sink. As he showered, the memories of the night and his all-too-obvious failings fell from his body and soul and gurgled away down the plughole, hopefully to be hurried thousands of miles away along the pipes. Removing himself from the cubicle, he dragged a towel over his weary body and climbed into his stripy blue pyjamas that had been draped ready over the radiator in the corner of the poky room. Gingerly, he began to tackle the stairs, creeping quietly up to the landing where he momentarily stopped and listened. He moved onwards to the end of the landing and silently turned a door handle. The bedroom door ghosted open to reveal the glow of a small lamp on a table in the corner. Fast asleep, smothered by a duvet, lay a young boy about twelve years of age. The duvet oscillated up and down as the boy's breathing gently raised and then lowered it as he slept peacefully.

"Goodnight, Stanley," whispered Sidney to his sleeping son, before retracing his silent steps backwards, pulling the door softly closed and moving across the landing to his own bedroom.

From his bedroom window, Sidney Rain witnessed the moon shimmering in the night sky and catching the white barcode lines on his stripy pyjamas. His tired eyes began to lose their focus on the rows of silent houses and gardens lined up in front of him. Sidney then turned around and allowed his aching body to fall onto his welcoming mattress. Within seconds he was fast asleep and the events of the night were forgotten, at least for the moment.

Chapter Three

FROM OUT OF the swirl of dreams and darkness, young Stanley Rain's alarm clock started to register. The repeating 'beep, beep, beep' prodded him out of his slumber. He could hear distant banging noises from the kitchen downstairs; his dad was up early, making breakfast as usual. Stanley yanked his duvet off his body and located his school uniform. Swiftly getting dressed, he manhandled his school rucksack onto his shoulder, brushed his brown hair out of his eyes and left his bedroom.

The kitchen was a hub of light, noise and activity. Stanley's dad, Sidney, was hunched over the hob chasing something around a pan with a wooden spatula, his blue-and-white stripy apron knotted around his blue-and-white stripy pyjamas.

"Oh, so the creature from the deep emerges," he greeted his son.

Stanley surrendered his school rucksack to the back of a chair and slid onto the seat at the table.

"You sleep all right, son?" enquired his dad.

"Okay, I think," Stanley replied, unsure as to whether he had or not.

"Done a cracking breakfast for you this morning Stanley lad. Bacon, eggs, sausage, beans and even a cheeky little tomato on the side; all as fresh as the morning dew. I only bought the tin of beans last Thursday." He heaved a spatula of beans onto a plate and crashed it down on the table in front of Stanley. "There you are my little ray of sunshine. Even that chef off the telly, Davie Oliver, couldn't come up with something as good as that," he said triumphantly.

Stanley looked back at him, confused. "Don't you mean Jamie Oliver?"

There was a pause before his dad responded. "Jamie Oliver. That's what I said." They both knew he hadn't.

Stanley clutched his knife and fork and began getting stuck into the fine cuisine on offer. After a few mouthfuls, he suddenly became aware that his father hadn't taken his usual position opposite and Stanley was, unusually, eating his breakfast alone. Instead, he was just stood there with his hands on his hips, trying to straighten his back as if he was in discomfort.

"You okay, Dad?" Stanley asked.

"Yes, fine, thanks, Stan. Think I slept a bit funny, that's all."

Stanley continued to watch him, whilst at the same time skilfully guiding part of a sausage towards his open mouth. Something wasn't quite right, he mused. His dad broke the silence.

"Stanley," he pronounced firmly, "I want to ask you something important."

"Yes Dad?"

Sidney hesitated for a moment before speaking. "Do you think I've put on weight?" As he asked this, he stood in front of the table with his arms outstretched, as if to make sure that the whole of his body was on view, even though it was wrapped up like a Christmas present in blue, stripy wrapping paper.

Stanley took his time before making his reply. He was wary of the need to be careful with his answer; how do you sensitively and gently tell somebody something that they don't really want to know? He eventually found a gap between the sausage that he was chewing on and the side of his mouth to utter a response, but even then he completely failed to find the words that were needed.

"Be honest, son. Have I let myself go a little bit?" Sidney asked while patting his stomach.

"Well… perhaps… a little bit… maybe… yes?" Stanley muttered hesitantly.

"Okay. All right," Sidney remarked in a resigned tone.

Stanley wondered whether he had given the correct answer, and was worried that he had upset him. "Dad, are you all right?"

"Yeah, probably just starting to feel my age a bit, that's all. Can't be twenty-one forever; been doing a bit of thinking and reading about changing my diet and getting fit." At this point he promptly reached over for his plate of fried breakfast and plonked it down on the table opposite Stanley. He continued as he squirted a huge spiral of brown sauce all over his food and wedged a forkful of bacon into his mouth. "I might try and join one of those gyms that they talk about; reckon five minutes of running on the old bread mill now and again and I'll be applying for the next Olympics."

"Don't you mean treadmill?" corrected Stanley.

"Yeah, that's what I said, treadmill." They both knew he hadn't. "What's gym membership these days? A couple of quid a year?" he asked as he slurped from a mug of hot tea.

"A couple of quid?" Stanley gasped. "Dad, it's more like about thirty pounds a month."

Sidney spat a fountain of tea out of his mouth and onto his breakfast. "Thirty pounds a month?" He carried on repeating it as he clearly couldn't believe it. "Thirty pounds a month! Thirty!" There was a pause. "A month!" Another pause. "Thirty pounds a month!" he said again, stopping to wipe tea off his face. "Can you believe it? Because I can't," he said, looking around the room in astonishment. "Blimey, you go to a gym and nearly kill yourself on the equipment, risk injury and all sorts, sweat like a pig and suffer intense pain and you have to pay thirty quid for doing so. World's gone mad." Thankfully, another swig of tea curtailed the sermon.

"What you can do, though, Dad, is get a friend to join too. You might get it for half price or something, or you could get someone you know to recommend you. Sometimes they will pay the person who recommends you as a reward for getting a new member in," Stanley suggested helpfully.

His dad abandoned his food and looked excited. "Yes, I know just the person. Terry Funk from work – he's bound to be a gym member, is Terry."

Stanley looked puzzled. "Who's Terry Funk?" he asked.

"Who's Terry Funk?" his dad asked rhetorically.

None the wiser, Stanley stared back. "Yes, who is Terry Funk?"

"You don't know who Terry Funk is?"

Stanley's eyes rolled around in his head, searching for a time when he had heard the name mentioned before. "No, I don't," he concluded. "Should I?"

Sidney Rain looked amazed at his son's ignorance. "Terry from the office at work. You know?"

Stanley plainly didn't know, and looked back at his dad in wonder.

"Terry Funk? 'Funky' Terry Funk? 'Uptown' Terry Funk?"

Stanley still had no idea.

"The Funky Bunch?" his dad continued.

Apparently, even this failed to register with Stanley. He stared back blankly.

"The Funk-Master General?" Sidney went on. "Sir Terry of Funk?"

"I don't know who you are talking about,

Dad," concluded Stanley. "Is he a friend of yours of something?"

"Yeah, he works in the office. He's one of the movers and shakers, is Terry. Right character, he is, and a right old laugh. He's probably just getting home now from a night out clubbing at the discos. He's bound to have done marathons and the like, has the Funkster. I think he swam the Channel last year."

"Has he won the Tour de France as well?" queried Stanley sarcastically with a big grin all over his face.

"Don't know if he's won it, but he's bound to have come in the top ten," his dad replied earnestly. "Terry's bound to be a gym-goer. I'll have a chat with him. Good thinking, Stanley, you obviously take after me in the brains department."

Stanley raised his eyebrows in response.

"So, anyway, do you need a lift to school today in the van?"

Stanley finished chewing and answered. "No thanks, Dad, I'm going to finish this and then head in early. I'm meeting Chloe and Billy at the corner and then walking to school. We want to get there a bit earlier today."

"Why? You been in trouble for being late? I've told you before about that Billy Bathurst. I'm not sure that you should be hanging around with him. That lad is a bit like the yoghurt we've got in the fridge." His dad's knife pointed to where the fridge was, just in case his son thought it might have been moved from its usual position.

"What do you mean?" asked Stanley.

"Extra thick," stated Sidney.

"Oh," said Stanley. "No, Billy's fine and we're not in trouble. We've got some new computers arriving at school and it would be cool if we got to use them first today. There will be iPads for us to use and everything." Stanley watched in horror as his dad used his knife to scrape the remains of baked beans and brown sauce from his plate before wiping the blade on his tongue.

"What do you need eyepatches for if you're using computers? Is it some sort of health-and-safety thing?"

Not for the first time this morning, Stanley was gobsmacked. "Please tell me that you mean iPads?"

"Yeah, iPads. That's what I said." They both knew he hadn't.

"Dad, they're like mini computers that you can carry around with you and take pictures and make films with them. They're really cool," Stanley explained. "It would be nice if Father Christmas got me one of those this year?"

"You and I both know that Father Christmas doesn't exist. Even if he did, I get the feeling that he's a bit short of cash this year. Keeping reindeers isn't cheap, you know."

Sidney got up and started clearing the breakfast plates off the table and plunging them into the sink.

"Blimey, my first computer when I was a kid was so big that we couldn't get it into the house. You best be careful," he continued over his shoulder as he squeezed his hands into bright pink rubber washing-up gloves, "I watched a telly programme the other day about how computers are taking over the world. Apparently, one day we will all be replaced by them and we'll all lose our jobs and everything."

Sidney Rain turned around from the sink to face Stanley with a serious, thoughtful expression on his face. "One day in the future, none of us will be needed any more."

The kitchen was empty. From the door there was a shout of "Love you, Dad" from his son, and a bang as it shut and Stanley headed off to school. Sidney stood there in his apron, pyjamas and pink rubber gloves with a small dishcloth in his left hand. The dishcloth dripped soap suds onto the tiled floor.

Before he headed off for work, Sidney Rain had a look in the downstairs shower room. His damp towel was still draped on the radiator, and he made a quick check to see that his Raven outfit was all safely tucked away and hidden in the cupboard under the sink. Stanley never, ever used this room, and so Sidney's secret remained safe. *Long may that continue*, he thought; the last thing he needed was his son finding out that his father was a crime-fighting superhero. Anonymity, in his line of work, was essential.

As he grabbed his keys for the van from the sideboard in the hall, he stopped to look at himself in the tall mirror perched on the wall by the front door. He studied the front view of his reflection and rubbed his beard, momentarily thinking about having a shave. Then he rotated ninety degrees and considered himself from the side on. He patted his stomach with the palm of his hand. Part of it was looking to spill out from above his belt, like a blob of custard left on the top of a jug.

"Fatman, indeed," he mouthed at the vision of himself. "There's life in this old dog yet," he concluded before striding out of the door and towards his delivery van, whistling a merry tune as he went.

Chapter Four

STANLEY RAIN SAW Chloe Scott bounding down the street towards the corner where she was meeting him and Billy Bathurst before they made their way into school a little bit earlier than usual to try out the new computers. For Stanley, three things were always noticeable about Chloe. Firstly, she had a shock of blonde hair that twisted at the sides, down to the top of her shoulders. Secondly, her school shirts were always whiter than white. It was as if she wore a brand-new shirt every day, or her mum popped it in bleach each night as soon as she got home and then dried and ironed it until it was perfect for school the following morning. Thirdly, and finally, he always noticed her smile, which could light up a room. Put simply, Chloe was the nicest person he had ever met. Stanley liked her because she was so genuine and honest. Chloe spoke her mind, which was usually kind and thoughtful. There were no hidden agendas with Chloe; what you saw was what you got. It wasn't that Stanley was in love with her, although if he were honest he would openly admit that he liked her a lot. Then Chloe was beside him, and her voice dragged Stanley from his thoughts.

"Would you look at him?"

For a moment, Stanley was confused and thought that Chloe was referring to him. Then he realised that she was nodding her head towards a figure in sunglasses over on the other side of the road. The boy was walking strangely, stopping every so often and looking back over his shoulder as if he was being followed.

"He's got sunglasses on, and it's cloudy with a chance of showers," Chloe pointed out.

Billy Bathurst marched across the street towards them, his spiky blond hair sticking up like porcupine spines above the jet-black goggles that he had wrapped around his face.

Chloe greeted him as if she were his mother. "What *are* you up to, Billy Bathurst?"

Billy raised his sunglasses so that they could see his eyes. "It's me, Billy," he whispered.

"We know," Stanley confirmed.

"What are you doing with those ridiculous glasses on?" asked Chloe.

Billy straightened up and looked both ways, as if what he was about to divulge was incredibly important and top secret. One of his typically tall stories was about to emerge. "You can't be too careful, Chloe," he warned; "you never know who's watching you."

Chloe and Stanley looked at each other, eyebrows raised simultaneously in anticipation of where this particular comment might lead. They both started walking, feigning that they weren't interested in Billy's latest fantasy adventure. He raced to keep up with them.

"Truth is, I've been working for the British government again over the weekend," Billy reported.

Chloe pretended she was interested. "Where have you been this time, Billy? Afghanistan? Iraq?"

"Not allowed to tell you, Chloe. It's classified top secret. Italy, as it happens. There are big problems in the Paris office."

Stanley and Chloe looked at each other. "Paris is in France, Billy, not Italy," stated Stanley.

"Wherever it is, I'm not allowed to tell you or I'd have to kill you," said Billy. "Do you like my sunglasses?"

No one replied, but Billy continued anyway. "They are indestructible. They're made from a titanium alloy, strictly government issue. I've got another pair if you want to borrow them. They gave me two."

"Why did they give you two pairs, Billy?" Chloe asked.

"As a backup in case I break them."

Chloe and Stanley looked at each other in exasperation. They both grinned, and the three of them headed towards the gates of Shigbeth Middle School.

"Put that down, Billy Bathurst, you cheeky little monkey."

Mrs Jeeraz was aiming her concerns at Billy, who, in the service of comedy, had decided to put an empty cardboard box on his head and walk around pretending he was a robot and deliberately crashing into the wall. Mrs Jeeraz's bracelet-festooned wrist jangled as she lifted the box to reveal a smiling Billy underneath.

"Stanley was telling us that one day computers are even going to take over from human beings, weren't you, Stan? How many computers have we got, Miss?" Billy asked, whilst applying the palms of his hands to his hair to get his spikes back into the correct position, which was always pointing straight up at the ceiling.

"I don't know, Billy, but there are lots and we have to get them all connected and ready in the next few days and you're not helping."

"Can't we stay here with you this morning, Miss?" he pleaded. "We could help you out, and between the four of us we could probably get it done in half the time."

"That's very sweet of you guys. Unfortunately, you all have to get yourselves registered in class promptly this morning. There's going to be a big announcement in assembly by Miss Tyler and we all need to be there."

"Wow, a big announcement! Perhaps it's even more computers or something?" Billy exclaimed.

"I wouldn't get too excited if I were you." Mrs Jeeraz frowned.

Chloe and Stanley noticed the resignation and disappointment in her voice.

"Something's up," remarked Stanley to Chloe.

"And if it's something Mrs Jeeraz isn't keen on, then the chances are we won't like it much either," Chloe added.

Chapter Five

EVERYONE FILED INTO assembly as usual in orderly fashion and took their seats. Stanley, Chloe and Billy were separated by different classmates. Chloe's hunch had been right; something important was going on. There was a subdued atmosphere in the hall this morning and Stanley couldn't quite put his finger on the reason why. Perhaps what was happening on the stage provided the reason? Miss Tyler, the head teacher, was stood over a lectern and was a little more watchful today than was usual. Normally, she was dismissive of the children entering the hall as if they didn't really matter to her and she was far too important to be bothered with the likes of them. Today was different. Her beady eyes darted out over the assembling students and burned into anyone who didn't find their seat quietly and without fuss.

Maybe she was trying to impress the strange-looking gentlemen who sat cross-legged on a single chair in the centre of the stage? He was a middle-aged man; very confident-looking and sharply dressed in a pinstripe suit with highly polished black shoes protruding from the cuffs of his trousers. His blond hair was greased back slickly over his head as if he'd just got out from a swimming pool and hadn't yet had the opportunity to use a hairdryer. He was smiling too, but not a nice, friendly smile as if he was happy to be at the school and to see the children. This was a smug kind of grin, as if to say, *I'm happy and I don't care what you think because I'm okay, thank you very much.* To Stanley he seemed creepy and unfriendly, and he wondered whether Chloe thought the same. Behind the guest, over his left shoulder, was a big blue curtain with a rope attached to it. Presumably, there was something behind it that the man was going to reveal to the audience.

Stanley's thoughts were interrupted by Miss Tyler's voice.

"Good morning, children," she said with a forced smile.

"Good morning, Miss Tyler," the congregation echoed back.

"Today is a very important day in the history of this school. For too long now, this school has settled for underperformance and simply being satisfactory. That is all about to change. When we return at the start of next half-term, we are going to be very different both in name and outlook. For about seventy years now, this has been Shigbeth Middle School." Miss Tyler glared at the children, as if seeking out someone or something that was hiding from her. "Some of your parents were educated here. Even some of your grandparents were once pupils at this school. That is all well and good, but we are not believers in sticking to the past. We are keen to modernise and look to the future; to be dynamic and to run like the wind rather than stand still with our feet in the mud."

Stanley took the chance to glance over at Billy, who was sat several students away at the end of the row. His mouth was wide open like a goldfish's and his eyes and ears were clearly straining to understand what was being said. Who truly knew what was going on inside Billy's head; if anything at all?

"It is essential that new values are embedded in a new school with personalised learning and understanding that is distilled from teachers to students, in a structure where opportunities are realised and robust systems are cemented to facilitate accountability."

Stanley was getting confused now. He and Billy were starting to look very similar.

"It is with great honour that I have the opportunity today to present to you our esteemed guest." At this point Miss Tyler's cold exterior seemed to slip for a moment. She gushed, and momentarily her cheeks went red as if someone within them had just switched a light on. "Girls and boys let me introduce you to Mr Nigel Greenstock."

The suited and booted guest rose sharply from the chair. Some of the students started to clap, but then stopped when they began to realise that this wasn't one of those claps where everybody was joining in.

"Thank you for that lovely welcome," he sneered. "Thank you too for that glowing introduction, Miss Tyler." The two of them flashed a sickly nod of appreciation to each other. "Let me tell you, children, a little bit about myself. I am Nigel Greenstock, the managing director of the Greenstock Clothing firm, an international business employing thousands across the globe. You've probably heard of us or worn some of our stylish clothes. We're very famous."

Some students shook their heads or looked at each other in bemusement. Billy started to fidget and began scrutinising his school uniform for any labels that matched the name.

"Greenstock are very keen to invest in a new generation of young people and foster all the core values in students that we all agree are absolutely essential in the modern business world; values such as resilience, grit and a determination to succeed."

Miss Tyler nodded her head vigorously. Stanley noticed that some of the teachers sat to the left of the stage either shook theirs or stared down at the floor. Mrs Jeeraz had her arms folded and looked as though she was having great difficulty in not shouting something out in protest. She was clearly not happy.

"Miss Tyler did say that today is a historic day for this school. Therefore, I am proud to announce that Shigbeth Middle School is going to change.

From September, for the new school year we will be known as Greenstock Academy. Preparations for this incredible event will start immediately."

He reached for the rope at the side of the blue curtain. Miss Tyler started to clap at an insane speed, and then stopped when she realised no one else was applauding apart from Richie 'Thicky' Drinkwater. The blue curtain drew back to reveal a large image of the new school badge with the name *Greenstock Academy* written large. Next to it was another sign with three words screaming out from it at the crowd.

"Let me introduce you to our new school motto: *Aspire, acquire, attire*." Mr Greenstock had a big, stupid, smarmy grin on his face. "Why aspire, I hear you ask?" No one in the audience had asked. "Well, we aspire to do better. No longer will lack of ambition be tolerated at this school. Why acquire, I hear you call?" Nobody had called. "Well, that's what we do at school, don't we? We acquire the skills that we need to compete in the modern business world. Why attire, you are thinking?" He was right for once. There were probably members of the audience, including teachers, who were thinking the very same thought. "Well, we at Greenstock pride ourselves on looking good; sharp of dress, sharp of mind, as they say! We want some of that Greenstock style to rub off on you youngsters."

Stanley noticed a bit of a commotion from behind the boards with the new badge and motto on. Two students nudged themselves onto the stage, with Mr Greenstock beckoning them into the limelight.

"It is therefore my great honour to preview our new school uniform for September, designed and made by ourselves at Greenstock."

The girl and boy waddled out to the centre of the stage in the striking new uniform. It was black with small white stripes running vertically from top to bottom. The new school badge was huge and covered almost the entire right side of the blazer. Stanley was relieved to see that the school motto hadn't been emblazoned on the back to make the students look like giant mobile advertising billboards. A murmur went through the assembly; a mixture of throbbing astonishment, intrigue and wonder. Stanley heard a student behind him remark that the pair on stage looked like zebras. Several correctly identified that the human mannequins were wearing something new to Shigbeth School called blazers. Another asked his friend if those were the same uniforms that prisoners wore in films. A hush descended as the models exited the front of the hall and Mr Greenstock and Miss Tyler came together to complete proceedings.

"Very, very exciting," exclaimed Miss Tyler. "Thank you so much for coming in to talk to us today, Mr Greenstock. No doubt we'll be seeing much more of each other in the weeks and months ahead." She lost her cool, went red again and giggled. Mr Greenstock cracked another greasy smile and slipped his hand backwards through his hair. "Dismissed," Miss Tyler barked, and the exodus from assembly commenced.

"I didn't understand any of that," quipped a puzzled Billy Bathurst afterwards. "Why was Davey Watts dressed up as a zebra?"

"Unfortunately, Billy, that's our new school uniform," said Chloe.

"But they were wearing blazers."

"Yes, and we will all have to wear them from September." advised Stanley.

"Ugh! I can't stand blazers. Still, I like the bit about things being embedded. I often find myself falling asleep in maths lessons, so it will be good if we are allowed to have a little sleep now and again."

Chloe and Stanley didn't correct him this time; after all, what would be the point?

As the three friends walked towards their first lesson of the day, the repercussions of the important announcements began to sink in.

"I don't like it, Stan," pronounced Chloe, who seemed very concerned by what had just gone on. "We've had no say in this, and surely we are going to be the ones that are affected the most by the changes? I don't know if our parents knew about this either. I'm not aware of any letters that have been sent home. I'm sure my mum would have asked me about this if that was the case."

"My dad usually throws letters from school in the bin anyway. Unless it's been on the telly, he has no idea what's happening in the world, let alone in Shigbeth," said Stanley.

"It just doesn't seem right, that's all. In a way, this Greenstock fella has just bought himself a school. Is that allowed to happen these days?" queried Chloe.

Stanley pondered the thought. "Bearing in mind what we have just heard in the hall, I think the answer could well be yes."

"Also, did you see the way that Miss Tyler was batting her eyelashes at him? It was so obvious that she fancies him. He's horrible as well, with his greasy hair and posh suit," Chloe added.

Billy was still trying to fathom exactly what the assembly had been about. "I don't get it, Chloe – why do we all have to go to church?"

"What are you on about, Billy?" she responded.

"Well, it's just that man said we are getting a new spire or something."

Stanley tried to set Billy straight. "He means *aspire*, not a spire. You know, as in being ambitious and wanting to achieve something."

"Yes, but he also said we were getting a new choir as well."

Stanley desperately tried to enlighten his friend. "Look, Billy, he meant *acquire*, not a choir. You know, when you get something like qualifications or high grades."

Chloe intervened. "You'll be telling us next that you don't understand what attire is either, Billy."

Billy looked hurt at that comment. The lines on his forehead screwed up and his nose twitched. "I'm not stupid, Chloe. I do know what attire is."

"Thank God for that," said Stanley.

"Won't be much use to us, though," said a resigned Billy. "None of us are old enough to have cars or know how to drive."

Stanley and Chloe shook their heads, and their mouths opened in wonder. They didn't know whether to laugh or cry.

Chapter Six

SIDNEY RAIN QUITE liked his job. Sure, it didn't pay all that much and the prospects for becoming a millionaire weren't great, but he never got up in the morning and didn't want to go to work. Someone once told him that was the perfect recipe for happiness. All right, he didn't get to see the world, but he did get to see a lot of Shigbeth town and the surrounding countryside. Being a delivery-van driver between different depots and industrial estates gave him the chance to get out and see what was around and also sometimes to meet some really interesting people. Above all, though, it gave him time to think, and this was actually jolly well useful for the other 'job' that he had; the work that he did occasionally at night as a crime-fighting superhero nicknamed 'the Raven'.

As the van rattled through the streets over the humps and bumps, Sid winced in pain. Last night was not a particularly good night in the history of the distinguished crusader against crime. He'd been outrun and insulted by a spotty teenager. Worse still, the Raven's pride had been dealt a bitter blow, even if he managed to get a couple of estranged chocolate bars off the pavement as a reward. For the first time in a long time, he was wondering whether he was physically cut out for this sort of thing. His back hurt and his legs were getting more tired, as the day drew on, from pressing the pedals in the van or marching parcels up and down driveways and stairs. Of course, he didn't head out into the shadows every night. Sometimes, weeks or even months would pass before he slipped on the trusty wellington boots and Raven outfit. Sometimes this was purely because of inclement weather or the simple fact that he didn't want to risk getting caught. A couple of years ago, reports of a mystery man stalking the streets wrapped in a black bin liner did feature in the local *Shigbeth Gazette*, but the tone of the reports suggested that the police were more interested in catching him because he belonged in a mental asylum as opposed to rewarding him for his endeavours or to offer him a job. He'd also been spotted by people on a few occasions too, so witnesses had seen him in full flow with cape and mask. One or two of the criminals that he had caught and left for the police had spoken of a masked figure who had been responsible for apprehending them, but they were soon dismissed by the authorities and labelled as lunatics or attention-seekers. Most of them didn't mention being captured by a costumed vigilante at all for fear of embarrassment. Even so, there were times when the Raven went into deliberate hibernation and laid low in fear of gaining attention from the media and authorities. The last thing he needed was to be caught and outed. What would Stanley think? Perhaps, in light of Sidney's recent poor performance, a more permanent type of hibernation or retirement was called for?

It had been a pretty normal day of deliveries, but when Sidney pitched his dilapidated old van into the depot late that afternoon, things became more interesting. As he pulled into the car park, there were no parking spaces. A fancy black sports car had taken centre stage by the entrance, parked where it shouldn't be, but a very attractive piece of machinery nevertheless. Furthermore, several of the other usually empty spaces had been taken up by new delivery vans. These were the latest models, all gleaming in black with silver wheels and not a spot of rust in sight. The name *Greenstock* was plastered across the back doors in fancy lettering, with the words *Aspire, acquire and attire* painted underneath.

Sidney Rain's mouth was wide open. "Wow!" he said. He ruminated over what he would do if he was given the choice of the fancy sports convertible or a new van, and decided that if he was forced to choose between the two, then the larger vehicle would win hands down. He tried to ignore the aches and pains in his back and calf muscles as he leapt from his van after successfully locating a space to dump it in. Maybe he wouldn't need the rickety old thing any more; perhaps one of the new vehicles was reserved exclusively for him? About time, he thought, for he'd had the old one for as long as he could remember working at the depot.

Such positive thoughts gave him a spring in his step as he bounded through reception and upstairs to the main office. The office was a huge open-plan floor with tens of workers at desks caressing phones whilst in conversation or stapling pieces of paper together in forced marriage. He stepped towards one of the first desks, where a bespectacled older man was busy licking envelopes in preparation for posting. He didn't have much hair on top, and what little bit of hair he did have had been carefully managed into a brown streak that chased down to his left ear. He wore a green cardigan that was buttoned up as far as it would allow, and a pair of beige slacks. If there was a competition for finding the dullest-looking person in the building, then Sidney may well have just won first prize.

"Funky, my brother, how's it hanging?" he chimed in greeting.

Terry Funk didn't respond. He carried on concentrating on securing the contents of his envelopes. Eventually he replied. "I'm licking envelopes," he said in a slow, monotonous voice.

"Yes, I can see that, Terry. What's all the commotion down in the car park? Somebody has left some flash vans and there's a cool pair of wheels on the double yellows at the entrance."

Terry's little tongue darted out, snake-like, and sealed the last item for posting. "We've been taken over by a new clothing company. Greenstock, they are called. Apparently, they are very big in the clothing world and need a new delivery section in Shigbeth. Oh yes, it's all very exciting." Terry didn't sound that excited.

"Greenstock! That was the name on the back doors of the vans. Magic! I'll probably be getting one of the new vans, then. You could come riding with me. We could wind the electric windows down, pump up the tunes on the sound system and attract the ladies," suggested Sidney. "We could go out clubbing together. You could take me to one of those all-night places that you frequent."

Terry Funk was perplexed. "What are you on about? What all-night places, Sidney?"

"Come on, TF. You don't fool me. Bet you're off out tonight, aren't you? Slipping the old dancing trousers on and wiggling away to some banging tunes. Captain Funk in the house!"

Terry wasn't getting through to his colleague, who was clearly under the misapprehension that this middle-aged, very mild-mannered office worker was some kind of disco diva. "Captain Funk, as you put it, will be in the house tonight as usual; *my* house, although I might pop out to dominoes at some point in the evening."

"Domino's, I love it; getting some pizza in before you go clubbing and burn off some energy. You can't dance on an empty stomach."

Terry Funk shook his head.

"Anyway Terry, I was going to ask you about gym membership – I'm thinking of joining one."

Suddenly, Sidney was interrupted as the doors to the director's office at the side of him were flung open and a slick, black-suited man strode into view, his greased-back hair shining under the fluorescent ceiling lights. He had a burly, suited assistant on either side of him as wingmen, each armed with ballpoint pens and blood-red clipboards. It would have taken someone with formidable audacity or a lack of understanding of the conventions of what was appropriate to interrupt these evidently important people.

Sidney strode over and offered his outstretched hand to the man in the middle. "Sid Rain pleased to meet you, Sir."

The suited man and his two assistants looked at each other in surprise.

"And who are you exactly?" the main man enquired.

"Sidney Rain esquire. Top delivery man of this parish. You've probably heard of me?"

They clearly hadn't. The two assistants leafed through the pages on their clipboards.

The boss spoke. "Hello, Mr Drain. I'm Nigel Greenstock, MD for Greenstock Clothing." They shook hands; Mr Greenstock hesitantly, Sid vigorously.

"An MD," Sidney remarked; "always useful to have a doctor around in case someone falls ill or trips over a parcel."

The two assistants looked at each other quizzically before one of them spoke up. "Mr Greenstock is the managing director. He isn't a doctor of medicine." Nigel Greenstock looked mildly embarrassed.

"So, what are the plans, Mr Bluestock?" Sidney enquired, holding the keys to his van right in front of the new managing director's nose. "Do you want me to hand the old keys in now?"

One of the assistants checked the papers fastened to his clipboard again. "Mr Rain, you say?" His fingers danced over what must have been a list of names. "Ah yes. Mr Greenstock, Sir, this gentleman is on the list; Mr Sidney Rain, a delivery driver." He prodded his pen and tapped at the name on the sheet in confirmation. "We aren't due to deal with these items until tomorrow, Sir."

Mr Greenstock looked Sidney up and down. He started at his scuffed boots with their worn laces, and his eyes worked their way upwards over the scruffy jeans and shirt that should have been cleaned several days ago at the very least. From there, he noticed that this man could have done with a shave and a haircut, too; the use of a comb wouldn't have gone amiss.

Nigel Greenstock's mouth opened to reply, while his eyes remained locked on his target. "Oh, I think we can make an exception here. After all, why put off till tomorrow what you can get done today? Right then, Mr Rain, let's get this over with. If you'd like to follow me back into my office. Please bring your keys with you," he instructed as he motioned back towards the door from which he had so recently emerged.

"Right you are there boss," said Sidney, following on behind them and sneaking a smile towards Terry Funk and a couple of other desk-bound workers, who had peeled their faces away from their paperwork in intrigue.

"Is that your sports car down by the entrance?" Sidney asked the director.

"Yes, it is indeed, Mr Rain."

"What type of car is it?"

"It's a very expensive one," Mr Greenstock replied, ushering Sidney through the door of his office and taking his place behind his desk with his assistants at either side like bookends.

Sidney didn't wait for permission before taking a seat.

"That's it, Mr Rain, make yourself comfortable. Please forgive me for the mess," Mr Greenstock apologised, flicking his hand at the mass of papers and letters strewn across the surface of his desk in front of him. "I often find that when you make a new acquisition there is a lot of clearing out to do; been busy this morning, as it happens, at somewhere else I'm taking over too."

Mr Greenstock took a moment to smile to himself and wiped the palm of his right hand across his blond, waxed hair. Then the smile disappeared and a more menacing look spread across his face.

"If you'd like to pass me the keys to your van, Mr Rain," he commanded.

"Right away," responded Sidney. "I can't wait to get rid of it, to be honest with you. It's not that useful any more as it's very old. It could do with a clean and it's starting to smell a bit."

"How very appropriate," remarked Mr Greenstock.

Sidney threw the keys on top of the piles of paper on the desk in front of him as he continued, "At the same time, though, it does feel wrong letting the old girl go. I've been driving that van for a long time. We go back a long way; feels sort of like a betrayal to just throw it out, so to speak."

"Well, change has never bothered me, Mr Rain. Throwing away all the old, decrepit traditions of the past and replacing them with something new, modern and dynamic. I have no sympathy for sentiment and what's gone before. That's the approach I'm taking with this firm. Bottom line is that I need a new state-of-the-art distribution centre, and this place and what has happened here before have no bearing on my plans."

"Absolutely, Mr Greenshot," acknowledged Sidney, his hands clasped together behind his head as he relaxed back into the chair as if settling down for a night in front of the television at home in his own living room. "If you just chuck me the keys to one of the new vans, then that would be great. I could even take it for a bit of a spin before I clock off for the day; that way I am ready to go first thing in the morning."

"Oh, please believe me, there are no new keys and there's no new van for you, Mr Rain."

For a moment, Sidney just sat there, not quite knowing what was going on. Then he suddenly realised, getting up from his chair and pointing at Mr Greenstock. The two assistants shuffled a bit closer to their master.

"Nice one boss, nice one. I get it now! You're a bit of a joker, aren't you? Never saw that one. You'll fit right in here, you will, with that sense of humour; can't wait to tell Terry and the boys that you nearly had me believing you."

Sidney was shaking his head and laughing. The two assistants, not for the first time that afternoon, looked confused. Mr Greenstock gave a sneer of contempt. He continued looking straight ahead, very serious and unentertained. Then Sidney started to calm down, and the realisation of what was actually happening began to register.

"Mr Rain, I don't joke around. I'm a businessman and deadly serious about all that I do. It's a recipe that works pretty well, actually; you only have to look at my shoes, suits and cars to see that I breathe success. I'm the complete opposite of you, Mr Rain; find a mirror and have a good, hard look at yourself. My success has come from being willing to make what some consider tough decisions, only I find them really easy. You're clearly a waste of space, Mr Rain, and I can't afford to have wastes of space in my company. As a hero of mine says on the television, 'You are fired.' Leave my premises immediately and close my office door on your way out."

Sidney tried to engage Nigel Greenstock with his eyes. He was suddenly upset and shell-shocked; looking at the director's assistants for signs that this was all part of some sort of joke, or confirmation that it wasn't really happening, but they just stared down at the carpet beneath them.

Mr Greenstock finished the conversation with a smile. "It's nothing personal, Mr Rain. It's just business."

Sidney didn't respond. He sloped out from the office without speaking, like the weight of the world had descended on his shoulders, squeezing his spirit and suffocating it. He crossed the workspace without even looking at the others at their desks. Even Terry Funk went unnoticed. Solemnly he walked down the stairs, and past the sports convertible parked on the yellow lines without even a look of admiration. He didn't even notice the kerfuffle now surrounding his old van because he'd accidentally blocked a loading bay when he parked it. As he started the long trudge home, even the earlier bursts of sunshine had submitted to the emergence of thickening grey cloud. Sidney Rain watched the first spots of rain begin to appear on the pavement by his feet.

Chapter Seven

THE MORNING CHIRP of the alarm clock interrupted the silence and Stanley rolled over beneath his duvet in a useless attempt to ignore it. As his senses slowly started to come back to life, he became aware that something was different in the house that morning. It was far too quiet! Normally, all the noise from the kitchen downstairs as his dad made breakfast would prevent Stanley from getting back to sleep even if he had wanted to. However, today things were eerily quiet. Was his dad up? Had he overslept? Was he even there? Hastily, Stanley started to assemble his clothes for the day and get himself ready for school before venturing downstairs, eager to find out why there was no banging of cupboard doors or clattering of pans.

He pulled open the door to the kitchen, and knew things were different straight away. There was no smoke or heat or spitting fat coming from the hob and no sauce bottles on the table.

"Morning, Stanley," declared his dad. "You sleep well?"

Sidney was stood by the fridge, clutching a bottle of milk rather than the usual frying pan. He didn't have his apron on, either. Stanley noticed that because his dad was wearing his stripy pyjamas and a couple of buttons were missing from the bottom of his top, so Stanley could see his belly poking out. Not a pleasant sight first thing in the morning.

"Yes," affirmed Stanley, "did you?"

"Slept like a baby," lied Sidney, banging the milk down on the table and causing the spoons in the bowls to jingle. Stanley guessed his dad hadn't slept well. He had dark rings around his eyes and desperately needed a shave. He looked tired; as if he had been up all night and hadn't had any sleep.

"What's for breakfast, Dad?" asked Stanley, eyeing the bowls on the table with suspicion.

"We're having a bit of a change today, Stanley, lad. We're having muesli." Sidney grabbed a packet and emptied some cereal into the two bowls. Stanley thought it looked like sawdust.

"Come on, grab a spoon. Splash some milk on and get stuck in," his dad enthused.

Stanley took his seat and copied his dad's actions with the milk and a spoon, albeit somewhat reluctantly. The two of them chewed at the muesli. Sidney made a face and a noise as if to suggest that it was really tasty. Both of them knew that wasn't really the case. Stanley thought that it tasted of sawdust too, not that he'd ever really eaten any.

"Why aren't we having our usual fry-up, Dad?"

Sidney responded while he was crunching away on his breakfast. A dribble of milk escaped from his mouth as he spoke and flowed down into his beard like a tiny stream.

"Well, I was thinking about what we talked about yesterday – you know, about me having put a little bit of weight on? I just think that we need to tone it down a bit and be more careful of what we're eating. So, it's out with the eggs and bacon for a while and in with the healthy stuff like muesli." He held his spoon aloft as if in triumph. "Anyway, you don't know all the damage that foods like that do to your insides. We don't want your veins getting clogged up with collateral, do we?"

"Don't you mean cholesterol, Dad?" Stanley corrected.

"Yeah, cholesterol, that's what I said." They both knew he hadn't. "All your top athletes eat muesli these days; that racing driver Lewis Hamilton does, and that Ronnie O'Sullivan who's ace at snooker."

"They're not technically athletes, though, are they, Dad? I mean, they're not runners or anything," Stanley pointed out.

Sidney thought for a moment as he chewed. "No, but Lewis Hamilton's still got to fit in his car, hasn't he? And snooker players have to spend all day walking around a table. I read somewhere that the average snooker player in one tournament walks hundreds of miles; enough to go from London to Los Angeles and back or something."

Stanley tried to change the subject. "Any chance of a lift to school today, please, Dad?" he begged.

"Sorry, son, but I haven't got the van today," Sidney replied, heading off to the fridge with the bottle of milk.

"Why not?" Stanley asked.

"I think that it will do me good to start walking to work and back for a while," his dad revealed. "You know, help get rid of some of this." He turned around from the fridge and patted his stomach. "Come on, finish your breakfast or you'll be late for school."

"I thought you were going to ask that mate of yours from work about joining the gym too?"

Sidney popped his pink rubber gloves on and doused his hands in the sink. "Yes, but it will be cheaper if I walk to work and back for a bit, and as you said yourself, Stanley, they are very expensive, those gym memberships, aren't they?"

Stanley couldn't put his finger on it, but something wasn't quite right. He forced down his last spoonful of breakfast and passed the empty bowl and spoon to his dad. Before he said goodbye, he noticed his dad staring out of the window, apparently deep in thought. No fried breakfast and now his dad being deep in thought. He was acting strangely, and Stanley couldn't as yet work out why.

Chapter Eight

SCHOOL THAT MORNING was unusual too. It was great. Mrs Jeeraz had unpacked and connected up all the computers and Stanley, Chloe and Billy had spent the morning with her, checking that everything was working correctly. As a reward, the three friends got to miss both maths and English. As the lesson before lunch was computing, too, they got to spend practically the whole day in the ICT room. They enjoyed the other class members benefiting from all their hard work, and Billy in particular was unusually focused, engaged and helpful. Even Mrs Jeeraz, who often spent time telling Billy off for messing about, was strangely complimentary about her new special assistant.

The only one who seemed a little bit distant and not her usual self was Chloe. She was still angry about the plans that had been announced the previous day for the school to be turned into an academy in the coming weeks. When she mentioned the new school motto of *Aspire, acquire, attire* she spat the words out as if they were poison. Chloe was aggrieved about two things in particular and they didn't even involve the new pinstriped black-and-white uniform. Firstly, her mum had known about the changes at school but had failed to inform her daughter 'because she wouldn't be interested in that sort of thing'. That really upset Chloe, who felt belittled by the perception from her own mother that she was too immature to consider such important matters. However, the biggest reason for her bad mood was the fact that her after-school basketball club on Thursday evening had been cancelled.

"You want to know why they've cancelled basketball this week?" she told Stanley, who had never even asked. "Because they are using the sports hall for a wedding fair, that's why!" As she informed Stanley and Billy of this, she thrust a leaflet in their faces.

"Cool. You mean there's going to be rides and stuff?" responded Billy.

Chloe went red in the face and Stanley realised that she was trying extremely hard not to hit him. "It's not that sort of fair, Billy, you idiot! Read the flyer here. It tells you all about it."

The leaflet seemed very slick and professionally produced; typical of Greenstock. Colour photographs of happy couples smiling and posing in dresses and suits filled the page.

"*Thursday evening in the sports hall*," Stanley read.

"Yes, they are cancelling basketball club so that they can start setting up for the fair. The leaflet even has our new motto on the bottom; it's verging on criminal," she complained.

"*Aspire, acquire, attire,*" mouthed Billy.

"They are taking over already, Stanley. That horrible man Nigel Greenstock is going to be in charge of this school sooner than we think. I reckon he's already wormed his way into Miss Tyler's affections. This school is starting to be run in the interests of him and his stupid company, not in the interests of the students, and that's plain wrong. We have always been Shigbeth Middle School and I want us to stay that way. I don't want to go to Greenstock Academy and I don't want to wear that daft-looking new uniform either."

"I don't like him either, Chloe. I don't want to wear a blazer," piped up Billy in support, "but I like the new computers."

"Computers are great, Billy, but they are nothing to do with Greenstock," Stanley pointed out. "Mrs Jeeraz said that those computers had been ordered weeks ago and they had just been waiting for the delivery to arrive. There might be more to follow according to her."

There was a lull in the discussion before an exasperated Chloe spoke up once again. "We can't just let this happen to our school, boys."

"I feel the same, Chloe, but I don't think there's a lot we can do about it," Stanley empathised. Chloe didn't disagree, but you could tell her mind was thinking of ways in which she *could* do something about it.

Later, in the computing lesson, the class were split into groups. Naturally, Stanley, Chloe and Billy teamed up, with Richie 'Thicky' Drinkwater making up the four required for the task. Each group was given one of the new iPads and the plan was that each team would spend the next few weeks in this lesson devising and producing a short film that needed to be 'of community interest'. At first, Billy didn't want to use the new iPads as he would have preferred to use the desktop computer that he had personally set up earlier that day with Mrs Jeeraz. The truth was that he had been set to work on that computer purely to keep him out of trouble and out of the way, but through a mixture of chance and accident, he had somehow got the computer working. Billy started to believe that this computer was his own special one; after all, it was a 'personal' computer, as he pointed out. Billy had always been into space and science fiction, and told the others that he had seen a movie about the future in which a computer had taken over a spaceship and started ignoring the commands of the astronauts on board. Billy even had a name for his computer; he referred to it as 'Billy 2000'. Unfortunately, for this task desktop computers like Billy 2000 were not to be used. Chloe came up with the idea of calling their group iPad Billy 2000 Junior, and suddenly, inexplicably, Billy's interest was rekindled.

"Why don't we do a film about space?" he suggested.

"Billy, it's supposed to be a film about something that affects the local community," Chloe reminded him.

"What about superheroes, then?"

Chloe was clearly becoming increasingly frustrated with Billy's proposed solutions. "Yes, because they exist," she remarked caustically.

"Yes, they do actually, Chloe. I've met one of them for real," insisted Billy.

"That bloke out late at night in a bin liner that you claimed you saw last year doesn't count, Billy," Chloe scolded.

"He waved at me."

That didn't impress Chloe. "I suppose you got your phone out and took a selfie with him as well?"

"I didn't have my phone with me," protested Billy.

"Knowing you, you would have held the phone the wrong way round anyway and taken a photo of the night sky," she chided.

"That was a real superhero, Chloe. He's called the Raven, and it was even in the newspapers!"

"Yes, and that's probably where you got the idea from to stir up your ridiculous imagination."

Stanley tried to change the topic before the discussion overheated. "What do you think, Richie?" he asked, optimistically turning to the school's least clever child to add his valuable input to the debate.

"We could do volcanoes," Richie suggested.

Chloe and Stanley looked at each other and decided not to comment. Even Billy thought it was a stupid idea.

"I think if this film is going to be about an issue that is affecting the local community, then we should do something about what is happening to this school," suggested Chloe with a steely look of determination on her face.

"That's not very exciting, is it?" Billy replied.

"It's not about doing something exciting, Billy. It's about doing something worthwhile; not everyone spends all their time reading comics. Some of us live in the real world." Chloe was now struggling to contain her disappointment with Billy, and her temper was rising fast.

"You're just upset because you can't play basketball," accused Billy.

"This is about much more than basketball, Billy Bathurst."

"Okay, Chloe, let's choose to do something really boring, then," protested Billy.

"Why, are you offering to be the star of this movie, since you're so boring?" Chloe struck back.

At this point, she grabbed Billy 2000 Junior and slid it across the table towards Billy. She then headed off to the far side of the room, found a chair, folded her arms, looked at the wall and sulked.

"Any ideas, Stanley?" asked Billy.

"Not really, Billy," said Stanley.

"Great. Looks like we're doing a local community film about a superhero that saves Shigbeth from an evil volcano, then," announced Billy, eagerly lifting Billy 2000 Junior from the desk and tapping away at the screen proudly.

Wisely, Stanley waited for a few minutes before wandering over to see if Chloe was okay. Fortunately, she had calmed down by the time he arrived and was ready to apologise immediately.

"I'm sorry, Stanley," she said.

"There's no need to say sorry to me, Chloe. It's probably Billy you might want to apologise to, even if he can be stuck in a world of his own sometimes. I know he can be funny, but he can also be really annoying too."

Chloe smiled, and her eyes welled up with tears. "It's not Billy who's upset me, or the fact that we are going to become Greenstock Academy. The truth is that I was really hurt that my mum never even mentioned it to me, presumably because I'm not grown-up enough to have a say in any of this or even care about it. She probably thinks I'm just a silly girl still."

Stanley was grown-up enough to know that sometimes you've just got to listen, especially when people are being honest about their feelings.

"You know I haven't got a dad, Stan. It's always been just me and my mum. I thought we were partners; I thought we talked to each other about things. I'm not so sure now."

Stanley knew just what she meant. "Well, I haven't got a mum, Chloe. Me and my dad are supposed to be partners too, but I only ever really see him at breakfast."

Chloe recovered a tissue from her pocket and wiped away a tear from her cheek. "I wish I had a dad."

"You can have mine," joked Stanley, "he's not particularly exciting. All he does is drive his van and sleep. He's even stopped cooking decent breakfasts now."

Chloe laughed. Stanley grinned. Mrs Jeeraz shouted. Billy stopped using the group's iPad to zoom in on Mikaela Franklin's bottom.

"I saw what you were doing, Billy Bathurst, you cheeky little scamp. We need to pack up now because after lunch you all have a road safety talk with Police Constable Green. We'll continue next time. Billy B, come and see me."

Chloe perked up a little. "PC Green's coming in this afternoon. He's lovely."

Stanley felt jealous for a split-second. Then he got up, helped to pack away and went with Chloe to lunch.

Chapter Nine

OVER LUNCH, CHLOE said sorry to Billy, who gracefully apologised too. They were friends again, just like that, as if no argument had ever occurred. Both Chloe and Billy were in a better mood because of the impending visit from PC Green. Stanley was less impressed than the others.

"He's not even a real policeman," he argued.

Billy contested that theory. "Yes he is. He's got a police uniform and a helmet and everything. He's even got a guitar."

"Oh well, he's definitely a policeman then, if he's got a musical instrument," Stanley mocked. "He's one of those community policemen. He doesn't catch criminals like on the telly; he goes around having cups of tea with old people, insisting that they don't let strangers into their homes, and doing talks about road safety to schoolchildren like us. He came in last year to talk to us about the importance of keeping dogs on leads. That was a complete waste of time as none of us own dogs."

"Community policeman, you say, Stan?" Chloe queried with a new degree of interest. "If he's interested in our local community, perhaps he can help us save Shigbeth School from the likes of Nigel Greenstock? And he's lovely," she added.

Mrs Jeeraz ushered the children into the classroom for the road safety talk and they each grabbed one of the chairs arranged in a crescent formation in front of the teacher's desk. The title slide of the presentation was projected onto the board behind the desk, and was emblazoned with the phrase *Stop, look and listen.* Sat in front of the board, facing the class, was Police Constable Green. His guitar case was prominently placed on top of a table to his left.

"You're right, Billy. He's a policeman. Check out the guitar case." Stanley's sarcasm was lost on Billy, who seemed really excited. PC Green smiled at the children as they sat down. Chloe blushed in response.

PC Green welcomed the class and started to make his way, in methodical fashion, through his presentation. He was a young policeman who even Stanley thought seemed to be a nice guy, although he wasn't quite the impassioned fan that Chloe was. PC Green was talking about how he felt when he had come home after a hard day at work, during which he had attended the scene of a road traffic accident involving a child who had been hit by a car outside school. He spoke very slowly and solemnly.

"Sometimes when I come home, I can't eat my tea," he confessed. "I tell my wife Bessie how sorry I am because I know she has cooked it for me. But I just can't face it. It's hard to eat when you've just spent the afternoon at the scene of an accident." PC Green shook his head and looked at the floor.

"Bless him," whispered Chloe into Stanley's ear.

Mrs Jeeraz felt that this was an ideal time for everyone to have a quick break. "Right, children, you've got a few minutes in groups now to talk about any questions you might want to ask PC Green before we finish," she instructed.

Stanley turned to Chloe. "I bet he hasn't got a wife. He's having us all on."

"What do you mean?" enquired Chloe, looking aghast at Stanley's suggestion.

"I'm sure that last year, when he gave us that talk about pets, he said his dog was called Bessie. I think he's making it all up. He hasn't got a dog, hasn't got a wife – I bet he lives on his own," Stanley insisted.

"Don't be silly, Stanley," replied Chloe. "Why would he lie to us?"

"You've got a lot to learn about adults, Chloe. Underneath that uniform he is still one of them," Stanley replied.

PC Green had by now recovered himself and order had been re-established in the classroom. Everyone settled down again. "Right – any questions, children?" he asked.

Stanley whispered in Chloe's ear, "Why do your dog and your wife have the same name?"

Billy put his hand up. "Have you got your guitar with you today, PC Green?"

"There's always one who can't keep his mouth shut," muttered Stanley, to Chloe's amusement.

PC Green then pretended that he hadn't brought his guitar with him. Some of the class shouted out that it was next to him in its case on the desk. Stanley tutted in contempt for his classmates. It was like watching the audience at a Punch and Judy show or a Christmas pantomime. PC Green pretended that he was surprised to find the guitar there on the desk. Unfortunately for Stanley, the case wasn't empty and as PC Green opened it, a cherry-red acoustic guitar was revealed. He sat back down on his chair and started to tune the instrument carefully.

"He thinks he's performing at Glastonbury," mumbled Stanley under his breath.

"I'll just get my guitar ready, boys and girls," announced PC Green to his audience. His fingers twiddled at the tuning pegs at the end of the guitar neck and he plucked at the strings, trying to get it to sound just as he wanted. As he did, he commentated, talking to his guitar as if it were a person.

Stanley whispered to Chloe, "I wonder if his guitar's called Bessie?"

"That's it… a little higher… there you go… yes… yes… that's it… a little more… yes… there you go."

There was a pause then, and the class thought PC Green was ready. He wasn't. "A little bit more... yes... think you're there now... there you go." Eventually, he was ready and the notes of a gentle tune started to emerge. He winked at the crowd before starting to sing.

"*Stop, look and listen. Listen to what I say. Stop, look and listen. Cross the road carefully.*"

He did this twice, and when he finished, the class clapped their approval.

"That was lovely," claimed Chloe.

Stanley was less impressed. "It didn't even rhyme," he moaned. "Since when have the words 'say' and 'carefully' ever rhymed?"

Billy raised his hand again. "Can you play it again, please?"

Stanley sunk back in his seat. "Please, no. Someone kill me, but only after killing Billy first."

PC Green responded with pretend concern. "I'm not sure, kids, because I've got to be back at the station soon."

A sea of hands and cries for an encore soon changed his mind. *Criminals all over town must be crying with relief,* thought Stanley.

The singing policeman launched into another rendition of his classic hit.

"*Stop, look and listen. Listen to what I say. Stop, look and listen. Cross the road carefully.*"

He did it twice more. Some of the children started clapping in rhythm with the tune, except for Richie

Drinkwater of course, who seemed to be almost deliberately timing his claps to fit the pauses between everyone else's.

Thankfully, certainly in Stanley's eyes, it was the end of the school day and time for everyone to go home. PC Green gently packed Bessie away in the case. Billy began pestering him for an autograph as if he was some sort of rock star. Chloe went up to say thank you. "I'm just being polite," she said to Stanley, who reluctantly accompanied her.

"Thank you, officer," said Chloe.

"It's PC Green to you, young lady. Charlie Green. And you are…?"

"I'm Chloe. Chloe Scott."

PC Charlie Green waited for Stanley to introduce himself too. After a short pause, he finally did.

"I'm Stanley Rain."

"Well, it's very nice to meet the both of you again." PC Green smiled.

"Are you a proper policeman?" asked Stanley. Chloe glared at him, as though the question was rude and inappropriate.

Charlie Green laughed. "Yes, I am a proper policeman, Stanley Rain."

"But don't you just give talks to children in schools and things like that?"

"That's only part of what I do, Stanley. I'm also doing lots of training and go out on patrol too. What I really want to be is a detective, and maybe if I prove myself then one day I will be." He suddenly thought of something, reached inside his jacket pocket and produced two business cards confirming his identity. "There you are, you two. There's your proof that I'm a real policeman. If you fear that any crime is taking place, don't hesitate to get in touch with me on that number there, day or night. I'll always respond straight away."

Chloe smiled and offered her thanks. PC Charlie Green waved his goodbye, hauled his guitar case over his shoulder and headed over for a quick chat with Mrs Jeeraz before leaving.

"He's cool," said Chloe. Stanley didn't comment.

They put PC Green's cards in their pockets and turned to find Billy. They eventually located him outside in the playground, swinging his school bag around and singing his version of PC Green's song at the top of his voice.

"*Stop, look and listen. Listen to what I say. Even if cars are coming, cross the road anyway.*"

Stanley turned to Chloe and grinned. "At least Billy's song rhymes."

Chapter Ten

THAT MORNING, AS soon as Stanley left to go to school, Sidney Rain had made himself a steaming hot mug of tea and plonked himself in his favourite armchair in the front room of 71 Bedlam Road. Suddenly, a nice cup of tea, his comfy seat and a spell in front of the television made him forget about the daunting predicament of having no job. Beforehand, his mind had been plagued with worries about what on earth he was going to do without employment. Where would the money come from to pay the bills? How was he going to get about without his van? What would his friends at work think? What would Stanley say once he found out that his dad had been made redundant? Sidney wouldn't be able to keep this a secret from his son for long. He slurped at his tea, stretched his legs out and flicked the channels on the remote to locate a programme of interest. There was a great choice this morning on the 'goggle-box'. He could watch families trading insults with each other on one show, or a house being auctioned on another.

It took him a good ten minutes before he realised he had become immersed in a nature documentary about the lives of penguins in Antarctica. It felt like he was on his holidays or playing truant from school. The minutes on the clock whirred by, and before long it was past noon and time for lunch.

He had some tinned tomato soup for his lunch and then proceeded to sit for another session in front of the television. There were only so many shows that he could watch about houses and antiques, and the quizzes that were on were no good to him as he couldn't really answer any of the questions. Boredom started to set in now, and the hands on the lounge clock stopped spinning round quite so fast. He watched them lumber around the clock face and realised that he had nothing to do; he even thought about doing some cleaning but that radical thought faded rapidly. He went for a walk about the house, popping into every room just for a look, just for something to do. The rooms were dark as the curtains had remained shut all day. He peeked around them to see if there was anything going on outside. He saw nobody, and nobody saw him. It felt like he was the only person left in the world. It wasn't as though he was in the mood for any company at the moment; his spirit had been sapped by the events of yesterday. He walked past the mirror in the hall and noticed that he was still in his pyjamas. His hands reached up to his chin and he stroked the growing beard that desperately needed some care and attention. He patted his stomach and marched upstairs to bed, where he pulled the duvet tight up to his chin. He stared at the wall opposite and listened to the silence.

There was a bang; from a door somewhere downstairs, perhaps? Sid tried to remember where he was and what he was supposed to be doing. He was in bed and it was dark. Not night-time dark, but the sort of shadowy darkness you get from curtains being pulled together in the daytime. He must have been sleeping. And that must be Stanley coming back from school! Sidney bolted out of bed and headed for the door. Then he realised that he was still in his pyjamas and a very quick change was needed. He pulled drawers open and slammed them shut attempting to extract socks, pants and a shirt. He pulled his jeans on around his ankles at the same time as he started walking. He tripped and fell into the wardrobe, which was open at the time. There was a clattering sound as his knees and elbows flattened boxes and shoes in its base.

"Dad, is that you?" called Stanley up the stairs.

"On my way, son," Sidney shouted back, clawing himself back onto his feet and fastening his trousers properly. "Just got back and getting changed. Put the kettle on for me, son, I'm gasping for a brew."

A few minutes later, he was back in the real world. Stanley was home and was opening the curtains in the front room as he entered.

"Blimey, Dad, have you been asleep?" asked Stanley.

"No, son, I'm just a bit tired from work," Sid lied. "It's all that walking to and from; I'm a bit knackered, that's all. Any road, where's my brew?"

"You want a cup of tea?"

"Aye, I put an order in from upstairs a few minutes ago. Did you not get it? Honestly, I've been out slaving away all day and this is how I get treated by my nearest and dearest!"

Sidney regretted being so bold with his lies, but the words had just come out of his mouth without thinking. He was desperate to avoid telling his son that he had lost his job. Stanley shook his head and strode off into the kitchen to fill the kettle. At that moment, there was a knock at the front door.

Sidney looked alarmed. "Forget the tea, Stanley, you get the door. It's probably one of your friends calling for you."

Stanley changed direction and headed towards the front of the house. Sidney hung around in the lounge, out of sight and listening intently for a clue as to who had come knocking.

Thirty seconds later, Stanley trudged back into the lounge. "Dad, it's one of those charity collectors – have you got any money?"

"Charity begins at home, son. Tell him to clear off."

"I can't do that, Dad. He looks really in need of

help himself. He looks like a bloke that's fallen on hard times," explained Stanley.

Sidney rooted around in his pocket and found a few coppers and half a packet of mints. "Here, give him this lot and get rid of him. I'll have to go round collecting money too at this rate, now I've got nothing left."

Stanley looked disgusted as his dad held out the less-than-generous bounty in his hand. He reached inside his own pocket and pulled out a gold one-pound coin.

"Blimey. It's no wonder I'm skint; my son's loaded. Look at that!" Sidney moaned.

Stanley sighed and headed off to the front door again. Sidney heard muffled conversation for a while. He didn't hear the door shut, but did hear Stanley's footsteps as he returned once again to the lounge.

"He's not going, Dad," Stanley reported.

"Can you believe it? Because I can't. He'll go in a minute when I put my size tens up his back passage. He's already robbed my son and taken all my mint imperials."

"No, Dad, you don't understand. The man at the door wants to speak to you. He says he knows you. I think you ought to speak to him; I think he needs help."

Sidney carefully poked his head around the lounge door and looked down the hall towards the open front door. There was a bespectacled man there with a blue cardigan on, beige trousers and a splash of dark hair fastened to the top of his bald head.

"Terry," muttered Sidney.

"Terry?" queried Stanley. "Uptown Terry Funk? The Funk-Master?"

"The very same," acknowledged Sidney, with a worried look.

Chapter Eleven

NOW THIS WAS going to be awkward, Sidney thought as he invited Terry Funk into the house. How was he going to deal with this situation without Stanley finding out that he had lost his job? Sidney escorted Terry into the kitchen and sat him down at the table. Stanley had started to make tea, but Sidney was determined to put an end to that and get him out of the way as quickly as possible. He seized the milk and cup out of his son's hands and popped them back on the work surface.

"Leave that to me, Stanley; I'll do it in a minute." He turned to face Terry. "You'll have to give us a moment, Terry, lad, I was just in the middle of something with Stanley here." He turned to Stanley. "Come on then, son, let's just finish sorting out that thing with your homework so I can have a chat with Terry here."

"What homework?" replied a puzzled Stanley.

"You know, that *homework* we were just doing before Terry knocked at the door," his dad insisted, placing special emphasis on the word 'homework' and nodding his head towards the kitchen door.

The penny dropped at least partially with Stanley, who followed his dad out of the kitchen.

"Do excuse us, Terry, we won't be a moment."

They headed towards the lounge, leaving Terry in the kitchen busy cleaning his spectacles with a white handkerchief.

Sidney pushed his son inside the lounge. "Can you go down the shops and get something for me, please?"

"Is that really Terry Funk in there, Dad? He doesn't look like the party animal that you described. He looks really ordinary to me."

"Stanley, the guy is clearly in some sort of meltdown. Have you seen what he's wearing in there? Lord knows what has happened with his hair. I need some time alone with him so I can get to the bottom of this. That's why I need you to go out. Why don't you get some chips from the chip shop for your tea?"

Stanley looked like he was considering the proposition. "But I haven't got any money now. I gave it to your friend."

His dad suddenly lost his caring tone. "What, you mean he's had it away with my imperial mints too, the cheeky so-and-so?" Sidney realised that this was something he shouldn't really be worried about at present. He needed to get Stanley out of the house and away from their visitor promptly. With a resigned look on his face, he reached into his pocket and pulled out a five-pound note. "Here, you can have this. Bleed me dry while you're at it, won't you?"

Stanley couldn't believe it. "You had this money all along, even when you thought he was collecting for charity?"

Sidney tried and failed to look innocent. "One of the top tips from your grandfather, God rest his soul in heaven, was that you should always keep your money separate. 'Use both your pockets,' he told me when I was a nipper. 'One pocket with a tiny amount in so you can always claim poverty, just in case emergencies come up like when you get pestered for charity or your wife needs a new dress; and the other pocket where you keep most of your money for other emergencies, like when you get a good tip for a horse and need to go the bookie's or they introduce a happy hour at the local pub. A wise man was your grandfather; he gave me lots of tips on life and that I am very grateful for. We'll gloss over some of them, mind, as he did do a stretch in prison. Now, do you want the money or not?"

Stanley recognised that he held all the aces in this little game. "If I had a tenner, I could get mushy peas and gravy."

His dad looked back at him, disgusted. "Stanley, you know I don't have that sort of money on me."

Stanley remained rooted firmly on the spot and folded his arms. Reluctantly, his dad pulled a ten-pound note out of his pocket, swapped it for the fiver and slapped it in his son's hand.

"Right, that's your lot. Bring me back a battered sausage and a tin of Diet Coke, and I want change or the sausage won't be the only thing in this house that's battered."

Stanley beamed, turned on his heels and left. "Be back in half an hour," he shouted as he closed the front door behind him.

Half an hour, thought Sidney. *Best get moving then.*

Chapter Twelve

"HOW ARE THINGS, Sid?" asked Terry on his friend's return to the kitchen.

"All right, my old pal. Yeah, good actually." Sidney hesitated, unsure as to whether to confess to his sacking at work. He made himself busy making the tea.

"Did you get fired yesterday?" asked Terry.

"More a sort of permanent leave, really, so yes, I suppose you could say that." Sidney forgot the tea and sat down opposite his friend. "I don't know what to do, Terry. I can't tell Stanley. I don't want him thinking less of me because I've lost my job."

"I know exactly what you mean," confided Terry, but Sidney didn't catch what he meant by that at first and carried on.

"All I've ever done is drive vans. I think I'm on the scrapheap now. Who's going to offer me another job at my age?" Then he stopped. "What did you say, you know exactly what I mean?"

Terry Funk lowered his head and sighed. "I got sacked first thing this morning too. Lots of us did.

That Greenstock character is cutting the workforce and bringing in loads of technology to replace us. The place is being revolutionised. We're all being replaced by machines and computers."

Sidney was genuinely shocked. "I thought it was just me. I didn't expect or want this to happen to anyone else."

Terry continued. "He called me a loser and said he just wanted winners at his company. The worse thing is, while he was telling me, one of his assistants cleared my desk and threw my stuff away; even my favourite stapler."

Sidney suddenly realised how hard this had hit Terry. He looked like a broken man. For a moment, he thought that his visitor was going to burst into tears right there at his kitchen table.

"I'm so sorry, Terry, I really am." He put a hand on Terry's shoulder. "I'll get you a nice cup of tea, mate."

The noise of cups and spoons colliding filled the uncomfortable atmosphere. Sidney started talking tough. "We should be doing something about this Nigel Greenshock character. You can't just take over somewhere, change everything and toss people aside like that. We've worked there for ages now; there must be a law against that sort of thing, surely?"

Terry still looked forlorn. "I don't know what I'm going to do, Sidney. My life's over." He took his spectacles off again for another clean.

Sidney crashed two cups of tea onto the table and took a slurp. "You shouldn't talk like that, Terry. We're British and we wouldn't have won all those world wars if we just gave up and let the French beat us. Let me tell you a little story about my Uncle Benny—"

"Did he lose his job, Sidney?" Terry interrupted.

"He lost everything, Terry. My Uncle Benny lost his job, his wife left him, and they cut off his gas, electricity and water supply. He was desperate and had completely lost the will to live, so one night he headed out to a bridge over the local river. He stood there for ages contemplating everything before he decided to jump off the bridge into the river below where he would drown and end it all. And would you believe it – at the very moment he jumped, a boat emerged from underneath the bridge and broke his fall, stopping him from landing in the water."

Terry looked amazed. "Wow, what a stroke of luck. So Uncle Benny survived, then?"

"For a few days, yeah, but then he died from the injuries he got after hitting the boat."

Terry looked confused. "So he didn't survive, then?"

"Not really, no," admitted Sidney.

There was a pause as they simultaneously drank from their cups.

"My point is, Terry, my old chestnut, that you never know what's coming around the corner or under the bridge, if you see what I mean. Something will turn up for us. You'll soon be back at the clubs with your disco trousers and dancing shoes on. I know you don't feel like it now—"

Terry tried to protest. "But I don't go dancing in clubs…"

"At the moment, no, you don't, Terry. Losing our jobs has hit us both where it hurts; in our pride." Sidney reached over and placed his hand on Terry's arm. "But we are not the sort of blokes to just cave in. We are Asda males, Terry, my son, and—"

"Don't you mean alpha males, Sid?"

"Yeah, that's what I said; alpha males."

They both knew he hadn't.

"Tomorrow, we are going down the job centre and we are both getting better jobs than the ones we've just lost, with better staplers and better vans," Sidney declared, inspired. "And when we do, we're heading back to the depot to tell that scumbag Nigel Greenblock exactly what we think of him. We're not the sort of people who just give up. When we get knocked down, we get back up again."

Terry smiled. So did Sidney. Even though, in a way, neither of them had much to smile about at the moment.

Chapter Thirteen

AFTER HIS CUP of tea and a chat, Terry left feeling a little better than how he had felt when he arrived. Stanley then returned with a battered sausage, chips and a health-conscious Diet Coke for Sidney. Father and son sat at the kitchen table and devoured the food, chatting and laughing as they chewed. It was just like old times; good times. Sidney momentarily forgot his worries and it was if he suddenly didn't have a care in the world. For a while he was oblivious to the fact that he had no job and, as a result, no money. Furthermore, his son didn't yet know anything about it.

As usual, Stanley went to bed at 9pm and was fast asleep within ten minutes. Meanwhile, Sidney flicked through the channels on the telly; a welcome distraction from thinking about his predicament. Stanley had always been a good sleeper. Even as a baby, Sidney struggled to recall a time when his son had been up during the night. He'd always felt perplexed when other parents commented about how tired they were due to their children repeatedly waking them from their slumber. Stanley had always gone to bed on time, gone to sleep quickly and never stirred until the alarm clock went off the following morning. Sidney could go into his room during the night and check on him, give him a goodnight kiss on his forehead and there would be no response from his son, who would be sleeping soundly and deeply. Clearly, this gave Sidney the opportunity to do what he wanted during the night, safe in the knowledge that Stanley would remain snugly wrapped in his duvet come what may.

A few years ago, it was during one of those long, quiet evenings when Sidney had first ventured out as his alter ego, the Raven. That night, there was absolutely nothing on the telly and nothing to do in the house either. Stanley was fast asleep tucked up in bed as usual and Sidney was wide awake, strutting around the house, bored and looking for something to do. He then thought he'd pop out for a bit and see what was going on. It looked dark and quiet out of the window, but Sidney was intrigued by the idea of what might be happening under the cover of darkness. Sure, some parents would be horrified by the idea of leaving their child alone in bed without an adult in the house, but when was the last time that Stanley had needed him or woken during the night? Besides, he'd only be out of the house for a bit, say half an hour; just enough time for a bit of an exploration and some exercise. *What's the harm in that?* he'd thought.

As time passed, Sidney ventured out more often and for longer periods. Stanley never woke up and never knew what his father was up to. And to be honest, Sidney didn't really know what he was up to himself at first. He'd walk the streets in the darkness through a world of relative silence. Sure, a few cars whizzed by now and again, the odd dog barked and occasionally, he'd see drunks stumbling home from the pub and homeless people twitching against the cold amongst the bins in alleyways. He wondered what these people would think of him walking the streets alone in the dead of night. He toyed with the idea of getting a dog so he could have a reason for his strange new hobby, but why should he justify it when there was in reality there were so few around to see him and he was doing no harm to anyone or anything? He was just going for a walk; it was as simple as that. And he enjoyed it too. It was fascinating to experience another world where Shigbeth was quiet and actually strangely beautiful. You could properly feel the weather and nature, and catch glimpses of animals similarly enjoying the safety and tranquillity that the night somehow offered and the daytime didn't.

That's not to say that things were always peaceful at night. From time to time, Sidney witnessed other things that went on under the cover of darkness. He saw fights between drunken youths, and lights coming on in houses where couples were having rows and voices and fists were raised in anger. And that posed the question of what to do. Should he intervene? Should he call the police? But wouldn't that lead to questions about what he was doing wandering the streets past midnight, looking into back gardens and through windows? What was he up to exactly when practically the rest of the more normal world was fast asleep? Then there was an occasion where he witnessed a man breaking into a house through a back window. Maybe he'd just forgotten his keys, or maybe he was intent on stealing items of value from those who were inside or away on holiday. Sidney hovered there for a few minutes, pacing up and down in the shadows at the side of the road, part compelled to act and part keen to run away as fast as he could and never go out at night again.

Then one night, he decided not to go out but to go to bed early instead. He tossed and turned, unable to sleep. Unlike his son he didn't seem to have the ability to shut down at the end of a day, respond to the beckoning call of sleep and head into the land of dreams. Eventually, he gave up trying and crept down the stairs, quietly even if there was next to no chance of waking up Stanley. He made himself a cup of tea in the kitchen and turned on the television. It was a film about a man with a cape and a mask who went out at night tackling crime. And as he watched the caped crusader watching the city from the shadows, his pulse raced and he realised that he had found his calling.

Within the month, he had acquired an outfit: a black cloak that swished in the air when he swung round, a pair of green boots and a large black belt. Then at a car boot sale he found a strange bird mask available for a pound. In his garage, he drilled holes in the sides of the mask and inserted cord so that it would rest securely against his face when he was running. On one nervous night, he headed out in his new uniform. Darting down roads and back alleys and hidden in side streets; away from headlights, street lights and prying eyes, he felt something he had never really felt before. He felt powerful. He felt important. He felt fantastic. Sidney Rain mattered.

One night, he watched a programme on the television about the Tower of London and the birds there that are believed to protect the Crown and the Tower. According to the superstition, if the birds are lost or fly away, the Crown will fall and Britain with it. This encouraged Sid to investigate these birds further, and the next evening he headed to the local library to find out more about them, thereby discovering that they are renowned for their strength and intelligence. This all fitted in superbly with the black uniform and the mask that hid his identity from the world. The Raven was born.

In the days and months ahead, the Raven went out every so often at night while his son lay sleeping and unknowing in his bedroom. Over time, he got to know Shigbeth inside out; all the roads and paths and alleys and back gardens. Sometimes he was seen, but not for long. Sometimes he saw a crime and acted. Mostly people just ran away when they saw him and there was no confrontation. Other times, there would be a struggle, some of which he won, others that left him with bruises and damaged pride. One criminal he even caught and tied up, hoping that people would find them in the morning and hand them over to the police. Nobody in Shigbeth believed anyone who told stories of a man dressed up in black with a bird mask, calling himself 'the Raven'. He made the papers on one occasion, when a CCTV camera caught a cloaked figure in a mask darting down the road. The Raven learnt his lesson. He simply laid low for a few months until everyone had forgotten about it. He noted the positions of cameras on his daytime delivery rounds so he could avoid them in future. He kept his night-time expeditions irregular, inconsistent and short. He knew Shigbeth town like the back of his hand. He knew where the darkness was. He was invisible to the world.

Earlier that day, Sidney had felt tired and humiliated. His legs and back still hurt from his failed apprehension of the thief the other night. His confidence had been shattered by Nigel Greenstock and his sudden sacking from the job that he loved. He had moped around all day, scared of being seen, a prisoner in his own house, hidden from the world behind closed curtains and a locked front door. Then Terry came around and showed him that he wasn't alone. There were others who felt like this too. If this could happen to a go-getter like Terry Funk, then it could happen to anyone. *We're not the sort of people who just give up. When we get knocked down, we get back up again*. Those were the words he'd said to his friend earlier that evening.

So as Stanley slept, Sidney looked at himself in the mirror in the hall at 71 Bedlam Road. He saw a man in black with a belt wrapped around his admittedly ample waist. His green wellies shone in the light. His smile went from ear to ear. As he headed for the back door, he slipped the bird mask over his face and gently moved out of the kitchen and into the back garden. He squeezed between the garage and the fence and out onto the driveway. His cloak swished as he moved, and the night absorbed him as he swept away from the house. For a moment, you might have caught a glimpse of a figure as he flitted past the back gardens at the top of the road. For a nanosecond a street light settled on his back; nothing more than a glimpse, or maybe even a figment of your imagination. Then he was suddenly gone as if he'd never existed in the first place.

Chapter Fourteen

IT WASN'T EASY tonight, climbing up the abandoned water tower that overlooked part of the town. Sidney Rain, aka the Raven, had clambered up the metal steps to the top on many occasions before. He had moved his mask to the back of his head and strapped a head torch around the front. It projected a little bit of light onto the steps and handrails to ensure his safety. When he got to the top, he stood on the balcony platform that wrapped its way around the tower like a lasso, switched off the head torch and took in an almighty breath. He used to climb the huge metal structure a lot faster, but he wasn't quite as fit these days as he once was.

The reason that he climbed the tower was for the view over Shigbeth that it offered from the summit. From there, you could normally view a whole swathe of the town in a 360-degree panorama if you strolled all the way around the balcony platform. Rows of buildings lined up in the distance like dominoes, with chains of street lights marking the roads in between.

Every so often you could make out the headlights of cars, like slow-motion shooting stars in the night sky. Most of the time there was very little going on due to the fact that it was past midnight and virtually the whole town was asleep. That made it very peaceful, and actually made Shigbeth town weirdly beautiful. The night hid the boring predictability of life in Shigbeth that you could plainly see in the daytime. In that way, it acted pretty much the same as Sidney Rain's superhero outfit did.

Tonight, however, the view from the water tower wasn't so great. Wisps of cloud obscured parts of the town from view; Sidney could see the rain underneath the street lights. The drizzle gently touched the metal tubes of the tower platform and rested on his cloak and the end of his nose. He'd been out for about an hour and perhaps it was time now that he headed back home for the night. The little bit of adventure had done its trick; he felt better and more himself than he had earlier in the day when he had lolled around the house and wallowed in self-pity. He took one last look at the town laid out before him and rested his gloved fists on each hip. He puffed his chest out and pointed his jaw at the sky in a proper superhero pose. Then, very carefully, in case his feet slipped in the damp, he flicked his head torch back on and started his slow descent down the steps back to Planet Earth.

The Raven flitted through the back alleys and lanes towards home, skirting along the edge of the allotments on Berrington Drive and at the back of the row of shops on Waterhouse Row. It was behind the shops that he suddenly became aware of a rustling sound near a huge metal waste bin and a tower of cardboard boxes. He stopped dead in his tracks and listened for more movement. The light rain drummed against his black cloak and rolled off in tiny waterfalls at his sleeves. He quickly reached for the head torch that was now clipped to his belt. He flicked the beam on and a circle of light appeared on the cardboard boxes at the foot of a wall.

"Who's there?" he demanded in a stern voice.

There was a shuffling of feet and a pair of legs emerged from beneath the boxes. A voice replied, "Raven, man, is that you?"

Sidney blew out a breath of relief into the chill night air. "Calvin, is that you?" he asked.

A bedraggled figure wrapped in an ill-fitting coat began to emerge from the rubbish.

"Yeah, man, it's me, Calvin. Just been trying to get comfortable, that's all. It's raining, innit?" he muttered, squeezing his eyes against the light from the torch.

Sidney relaxed. Calvin was one of the homeless men that he sometimes met on his travels. He tended to move from place to place in Shigbeth and sleep out in the open. Usually, he'd be in a bus shelter or inside the wooden pirate ship on the children's playground over near Warchester Park. When it was cold, he would find a shed in a back garden and camp there for the night, or even for the whole day if it was particularly chilly.

"How are you, my friend?" asked Sidney.

"I'm good, man. Was just getting out of the rain for the night and found this top-quality cardboard." Calvin looked tired. His skin was crumpled up like a once-pristine piece of paper that had been screwed up into a ball, thrown away and then retrieved and unfolded again. His shoes had no laces and he wore a stripy bobble hat. As he talked, he waved his arms and the bobble danced about at the sides of his head. He'd been drinking.

"You been fighting crime tonight, Mr Raven?" he enquired, wobbling on his feet.

"Not tonight, Calvin. Think it's the rain; keeps the bad guys inside."

"Yeah, and the good guys outside," remarked Calvin, gesturing at himself and Sidney. There was very little chance of Calvin reporting the existence of the Raven to the authorities. Nobody would believe the word of a homeless drunk.

"You got any information for me, Calvin?" asked Sidney. Whenever he met Calvin, he would play out a little scene whereby Calvin would feed him a bit of information for a small fee. None of the information was ever true, but it was a way in which Sidney could help him out a little bit.

"Let me see now." Calvin stroked his scruffy grey beard as he thought and the scene started to unfold.

The Raven reached into his pocket and found a silver coin. As he did this, Calvin's memory miraculously recovered. Sidney pressed the money into Calvin's hand.

"Ah yes, you might want to check out by the school, Mr Raven, man. There's something going on there tonight; big delivery truck, sir."

"Thanks, my good friend," acknowledged the Raven.

"Thanks to you, sir," Calvin replied, holding the coin up to the light from the head torch as if checking it was real and not made of chocolate. "And you can rest assured, Mr Raven, that I will be investing this money very wisely. It'll be going straight into my savings account at the building society first thing tomorrow morning, yes sir. You won't find me spending this money in the off-licence down on Frobisher Street. It doesn't open until ten in the morning these days anyway, since the management there changed."

Sidney raised his eyes in dismay. Calvin disappeared head first into a cardboard box. "Night, Mr Raven, sir," he called.

"Goodnight, my loyal friend," responded Sidney. He dreamed that one day he would come back to Calvin with thousands of coins, and he would take him away from here and pay for him to get better.

Sidney had stopped listening to Calvin and his priceless bits of information a long time ago. The first few times, he'd keenly followed the tip-offs, caught up in the excitement and adventure. He soon realised that they led nowhere and Calvin was just making things up off the top of his head to gain money to spend on his drink habit. Tonight, however, Shigbeth School was on a shortcut that Sid knew would take him home anyway, so he hastily walked off in that direction, eager by now to get out of the drizzle.

The Raven moved in the shadows along the garages at the side of the school where Stanley was a pupil, and down a path at the back of the houses that ran along the trees bordering its perimeter. As he got closer to the school, he noticed lights on in the building by a side entrance. Strange, he thought; why would the lights be on at this time of night? Maybe they'd accidentally been left on by the caretaker, which wasn't particularly good news for whoever was paying the electricity bill. But as he hugged the treeline which moved diagonally towards the building, he heard noises and could see a large van parked up against the building. The doors at the back of the vehicle appeared to be open, and Sidney was sure that he could see movement in the shadows between the doors and the building. Something unusual and very suspicious was going on. He forgot the rain and his plans to go home, pushed his right fist into his left palm and readied himself for action. His pulse quickened in response as he crept forwards for a better view.

He got as near as he could, using the trees as cover, but he still couldn't see exactly what was going on. There was a wall lining a series of back gardens to his right. If he could somehow climb up on top of the wall, he would have a much better view and be able to work out precisely what was going on. He inched over to the wall, keeping out of sight, his brain whirring in the search for ideas. A dustbin invited a route onto the wall and he very carefully climbed on board, using his arms to stay balanced once he had two feet on top. Worried that it would collapse under his weight, he then used his arms and knees to mount the brick wall as if he were hoisting himself out at the side of a swimming pool. Then, clutching the top of the wall for dear life, he managed to steady himself and slowly shuffle along towards the best viewpoint. Carefully, he bent at the knee and pulled himself up onto his feet, making sure he didn't trap his cloak underneath his boots and propel himself forwards head first onto the ground below. He stretched his arms out for balance, looking like a bird about to take flight. With a deep breath, standing on the wall, his concentration now focused on the scene outside the school before him. He could make out two men shuttling back and forth between the school building with the lights on, and the open doors at the back of the van. Boxes were clutched to their chests. At first, Sidney pondered whether they might be making deliveries to the school in the middle of the night. However, it definitely appeared that the men were taking the boxes from the school and loading them into the gaping jaws of a getaway vehicle.

"This is theft," he muttered under his breath. Hundreds of thoughts raced through his mind. Calvin had been right for the first time ever. This could be the Raven's biggest crime-fighting feat. But there were two of them – how could he tackle them both at the same time? Shouldn't he phone the police or cry for help? He didn't have a phone. Shouldn't he be home by now anyway? And how was he going to get down from this wall? Suddenly, a single thought flashed into his brain, emerging from the maelstrom of others. The van doors closed and the light from the school building lit up the back of the vehicle and revealed the two thieves who were close to completing their night's work.

"My God," mouthed the Raven. In that moment, he stepped back a little bit too far and placed his left foot off the wall and into thin air. Gravity took effect and did the rest. The world started to spin as he tumbled backwards into the garden on the other side. The darkness seemed to swirl round him before he hit the ground with a crunch. Then the blackness enveloped him completely.

Chapter Fifteen

HE AWOKE, AND straight away felt something wet splashing on his face. *Still raining?* he wondered. Then he realised it wasn't rain. His face was being licked by a dog. He sat bolt upright and panicked.

"Come away, Scruffles," someone called.

Sidney tried to get away from the flashing tongue of the dog licking his face and work out where on earth he was and how he had got there. He wiped his face with a gloved hand and realised he was sat in a garden amidst a selection of plants and bushes.

"Scruffles, leave the man alone, will you?" said a voice.

There was an old man over by the back door of the house, trying to encourage obedience from his little terrier, apparently named Scruffles.

"You fell off the wall," the old man confirmed.

Sidney looked at the wall behind him and remembered something about being on top of it – perhaps trying to take a shortcut home? He rubbed the back of his head and grasped his shoulder.

"Looks like you've banged your head," suggested the man, who now had his pet under control and sniffing at his slippers.

Sidney looked up, confused. It was still raining a little. He had soil in his mouth and he felt a bump on the back of his head.

"I was just about to let Scruffles out for a wee when I saw you fall from the wall."

There was a pause as they looked each other up and down. Sidney saw that the man was in his pyjamas with a ruby-red dressing gown tied around him.

"Have you been fishing?" asked the man.

That didn't help the confusion. "Err... yes?" Sidney responded in quizzical fashion, not really knowing what the old man meant.

"You've got wellies on and a blanket around you, so I figured that you've been night fishing. Your torch is by your feet too, I notice. Were you trying to take a shortcut home?"

Sidney groaned as he staggered to his feet, still rubbing the bruise at the back of his head. "Yes, I guess I was," he muttered, looking back at the wall and wondering what on earth he had really been up to.

"Where's your rod?" asked the man. By now Scruffles had lost interest and was going to the toilet in the middle of the lawn.

Sidney searched for an answer to the question. "I must have left it at the lake. I'd probably best go back and get it."

The old man looked puzzled too. "Not many lakes around here, young man," he pointed out.

Again, Sidney racked his muddled mind for an answer, but this time to no avail. "Not really, no," was all he could manage to offer.

The old man walked over to him and put a helpful hand on Sidney's arm to steer him towards the gate. "Are you sure you are okay? Bit of a nasty fall, that."

Sidney followed the old man's lead and gingerly moved with him towards a gate. "Thank you," he said politely.

"No problem, young man. Hope you get your fishing rod back. Perhaps you should be a bit more careful climbing up walls in future?"

"I will," Sidney promised as he shuffled out of the opened back gate. "Thanks for your help."

"Not to worry," said the man, "we all need a little bit of help sometimes. We can't always be doing everything by ourselves like we used to."

Sidney was on the back lane by a line of trees next to Shigbeth School. He heard the gate being bolted behind him and the old man congratulating Scruffles for doing a poo in the middle of his lawn. Sidney rubbed his head, checked he had everything including his mask and torch, and began to amble home in the direction of Bedlam Road. As he heaved his aching body along, he realised that he couldn't really remember much of the evening. He recalled being at the water tower, but after that, virtually nothing.

But as he slowly made his way home to Stanley, there was something very important that he remembered from his apparent adventure that night. The old man's words echoed in his head: *We all need a little bit of help sometimes. We can't always be doing everything by ourselves like we used to.* His last two outings as the Raven were trying to tell him just that. He couldn't physically do this like he used to; being outrun and ridiculed by a teenager and falling off a wall with no idea what he was doing climbing it in the first place. Like the old man had said, perhaps there is a time when we have to accept cold reality, admit the limits of our capabilities and seek help. After all, Batman did have Robin and Superman did have Supergirl. Maybe the Raven needed a partner, a sidekick; this wasn't a job for a single person any more. He needed someone with bravery coursing through their veins, a man of action with nerves of steel, someone who knew the way of the world and was fine with being active at night. He needed someone who also needed a purpose and something new into which to channel their energies. Sidney thought he knew just the man who could help him.

Chapter Sixteen

THE NEXT MORNING, Stanley called round for Chloe on the way to school. She had obviously seen him coming as she appeared at the door before he'd even pushed the latch down on the wrought-iron gate that led to the front garden. Chloe gave her mum a big hug and then skipped down the path to join Stanley on the pavement.

"I see you have made up with your mum, then," observed Stanley.

"Yes, I did." Chloe beamed a huge smile. "We had a really good chat last night and she apologised for not talking to me about the plans for the school. She agreed that because I'm older, I deserve treating a little bit more like an adult, and that we'll make important decisions together in future."

Stanley smiled back. "Good. I'm glad things are better, Chloe. You were really upset yesterday."

"I know, but I'm fine again now," she confirmed. "I've decided that I am going to get one of the iPads and do a film about what's happening to our school.

My mum says that if you think something in life is unfair, then you need to do something about it rather than just sit there doing nothing. We talked about people like Martin Luther King; it was like a little history lesson. Did you talk to your dad about it?"

The truth was that Stanley hadn't bothered to talk to his dad about what was happening at school, what with Terry Funk arriving on the scene during the evening. He was a bit embarrassed as he didn't want Chloe to think that he wasn't taking it seriously.

"Sorry, Chloe, I didn't get the chance last night. Dad had a friend round so we didn't really see each other. I haven't seen him this morning either. He's staying off work today with a bad back, so he's still in bed." The final bit was certainly true. Stanley hadn't even seen his dad at breakfast that morning as he lay in bed groaning instead of coming downstairs. In his apparent agony, he'd still managed to put in a request for a cup of tea, though, with Stanley kindly obliging and marching up the stairs with his order.

"If you ask me, he's taking that healthy-living thing far too seriously," said Chloe. "You can't just start exercising all of a sudden at that age and expect your body to cope."

"As far as I can tell, he hasn't started exercising yet. Him and his mate Terry still haven't joined a gym," replied Stanley.

"But he's doing all that healthy-eating stuff though,

isn't he? Did you have muesli for breakfast again this morning?"

Stanley rubbed his tummy. "No, I couldn't face it. It looks like something that's left over when you've been cleaning out a budgie cage. I'm starving."

Chloe giggled.

"And anyway, he had a battered sausage, chips and a Diet Coke for his tea last night, so he's hardly eating healthily round the clock, is he?"

"No, but at least he's opting for a Diet Coke to go along with his sausage and chips," she pointed out. "It's a start."

Stanley was just about to tell Chloe all about the unexpected visit from Terry Funk last night, when she interrupted his train of thought.

"It's Billy," she shouted.

Sure enough, heading towards them, walking away from school, was Billy. His red rucksack was slung over his shoulder and his spiky blond hair bobbed along with the rhythmic drumming of his feet on the pavement.

"Yo, losers!" he called.

"Good morning, Billy," Chloe greeted him politely.

"You're going the wrong way," Stanley informed him.

"School's closed today." Billy grinned.

"Yeah, course it is, Billy," said Chloe, preferring to ignore their friend's breaking news.

"It is, honestly."

"Come on, Stanley, let's go; we're not falling for that one."

Billy looked aggrieved that his friends didn't believe him. His face twitched in disbelief that they didn't trust what he told them. "Go and see for yourself, then. There are police cars and ambulances and fire engines at the school gate," he urged.

"Is there a helicopter too?" asked Stanley sarcastically.

"Not that I could see," responded Billy.

Stanley and Chloe glanced at each other.

"It's true, I swear it." Billy opened his arms out to his friends as if intimating that he had absolutely nothing to hide.

"We'll go to school anyway and just check," decided Chloe.

"Fine," replied Billy, "don't believe me, then. I'm going home."

He pulled his rucksack up over his shoulder and bounced down the street in the opposite direction to the one in which he should have been going. He turned his head and grinned over his shoulder. As he did this, he didn't notice a raised paving slab and tripped over, only just managing to keep his balance and his pride intact.

Chloe and Stanley laughed. "He's really going home, you know," noted Chloe. The two of them turned and headed for school.

Chapter Seventeen

FOR PROBABLY THE first time in his life, Billy Bathurst wasn't lying. Well, at least partly. When Chloe and Stanley rounded the corner towards the school gates, there were no ambulances, fire engines or indeed helicopters, but there were two police cars in the car park; one even had its blue lights flashing. An almighty kerfuffle was going on. Miss Tyler was out of her office for once and was directing arriving pupils. PC Green was there talking to worried parents. There was even a man there still in his pyjamas and red dressing gown, walking his dog and nosily hanging around to see what the excitement was all about. As Stanley and Chloe slowly moved through the chaos with mouths wide open in astonishment, they saw Mrs Jeeraz urging boys and girls to move into the school and away from the action.

"Billy says that the school is shut, Miss," called Chloe.

Mrs Jeeraz's normally happy expression turned immediately into a frown. "And do you, Chloe Scott, always believe everything that cheeky little monkey says to you?"

Chloe and Stanley looked at each other. "So school's still open, then," concluded Stanley.

"Yes, it most definitely is," Mrs Jeeraz replied. "Come on in, students," she called out.

"What's happened?" asked Stanley. "Why are the police here?"

"We've had a break-in during the night, Stanley. Someone has broken into the school and taken all the computers."

"The new ones?" asked Stanley.

"The new ones," confirmed Mrs Jeeraz.

"Wow! Including the iPads?" enquired Chloe.

"Everything, Chloe – they've taken the lot."

Mrs Jeeraz headed off to herd more children away from the car park and into the school. PC Charlie Green appeared next to Chloe and Stanley.

"Hi, Constable Green," said Chloe excitedly.

"Hi there, young Chloe," he responded, clearly recognising her from yesterday afternoon.

"There's been a break-in, then?" she enquired.

"Well, no, there hasn't actually," he corrected.

"What do you mean?" asked a puzzled Stanley. "Mrs Jeeraz just said there has been."

Constable Green tipped his head from side to side as he attempted to clarify the situation. "What I mean is that no one has strictly broken in. No windows were smashed and no locks were broken. It's almost as if the computers have completely vanished into thin air."

"So what happens now?" Chloe asked.

"Well, we will talk to all the teachers and also the neighbours to see if we can find anything out. But apart from that there isn't a lot we can do. There is no evidence, you see."

"What about fingerprints?"

"There aren't any, Chloe. Whoever came in was well prepared and probably wore gloves. There's no sign of anybody coming in or out of the building."

Stanley's brain was doing overtime. His dad watched lots of detective shows on the telly and so he felt he knew crime-solving procedures pretty well. "What about closed-circuit TV cameras – we must have them in school, surely?"

PC Green shook his head. "I'm afraid not. The school hasn't got any at the moment, but I will be recommending that it gets some fixed up at some point in the future."

"Not a lot to go on then, Constable Green," Chloe summarised.

"I don't think we'll be solving this crime in a hurry, if I'm honest," sighed PC Green with a look of defeat evident on his face. "Still, I gave you my card yesterday, kids, so if you see or hear anything just call me any time, day or night." He tipped his helmet towards Chloe and Stanley.

His attention was then diverted to an approaching

Miss Tyler, her high heels scraping the concrete as she shuffled towards them.

"Chloe and Stanley please leave this young policeman alone while he conducts his very important enquiries," she sneered, giving the children a cold look. Chloe was about to complain, but fortunately her response was cut off by PC Green.

"Don't worry, Miss Tyler. Chloe and Stanley were actually trying to see if there was anything they could do to help."

Miss Tyler's cold stare didn't change at all. Most teachers would smile and be heartened by the news of two children reacting to a call of duty and doing their selfless best in service for their local community. She just raised her eyebrows as if she didn't believe what she had just been told.

"That's all well and good but I really think it's about time you two got yourselves into school and got on with your lessons. I'm sure Officer Green has a lot of work to do at the moment as he investigates." Miss Tyler stood waiting for Chloe and Stanley to move. It even looked like PC Green felt he was getting a telling-off too. He shuffled his feet and started to move away.

"Righto, will do," he announced, turning around, eager to find someone to talk to in order to signal that he was taking the investigation of this crime very seriously indeed.

Miss Tyler stared at Chloe and Stanley, awaiting

their response. Even Chloe decided it would be unwise to protest, and she turned and headed inside to the classroom. Stanley followed, not saying a word for fear of inviting the head teacher's wrath.

Chapter Eighteen

LATER ON THAT morning, Stanley and Chloe's class were about to start their lesson. This time was usually reserved for working with IT, but unfortunately, because of the theft there were no computers left in school for the pupils to use. Instead, Mrs Jeeraz gave out some old, battered textbooks about the world of business.

"Miss Tyler has said that as we have no computers at the moment, we are going to have to do some business studies as an alternative. This is something we are going to be doing more of at this school in future anyway."

Chloe turned to Stanley and whispered, "Business studies! I knew it! This will all be related to the fact that we are becoming Greenstock Academy."

Stanley wasn't entirely sure what she was getting at. Chloe continued with her theory.

"That slimeball Greenstock wants to turn us all into business people just like him, and this is part of the brainwashing."

"I'm not sure about that, Chloe," Stanley said. "We're only doing this because the computers have been stolen."

"Believe me Stanley, this is all part of the plan. We'll all be working down his factory before the end of next year. We've got our new uniforms on order, we can't do sport because our hall is being used for a wedding fair to make him money, and now we are being handed out the lines we've got to learn in these textbooks."

Stanley didn't argue. Chloe wasn't in the mood for alternative viewpoints. He opened the textbook and followed the instructions that Mrs Jeeraz was busily writing on the whiteboard.

Chloe nudged him and nodded at something going on out of the window. Stanley peered outside, across the yard to the cloakroom doors. Miss Tyler was there. So was Billy, whose day off from school clearly hadn't lasted long. There was a tall gentleman with them who had curly grey hair.

"Must be his dad," said Chloe.

A few minutes later, Billy was delivered to the classroom. He was guided to his seat by Miss Tyler, who took the opportunity to look around the room with a glare of disapproval, inviting anyone who dared to catch her eye. Billy sat down opposite Stanley and Chloe. Miss Tyler exited the room and everyone relaxed a little.

"What are we doing?" asked Billy.

Stanley nodded at the textbook in front of Billy, who read the title on the front cover.

"Business studies!" he exclaimed. He raised his hand in the air and turned his head around to face Mrs Jeeraz. "Do we have to do this, Miss?" he protested. "I'd rather do geography and that's rubbish."

Mrs Jeeraz sighed. "We have to do this, Billy Bathurst, because all our computers have been stolen."

Billy turned to look at Chloe. "Is that why the police were here this morning and school was closed?"

Chloe sighed as well. "Yes, that's why the police were here, and no, school wasn't closed, Billy, in spite of what you think."

"Are all the new computers gone?" he asked.

"Yes, Billy," said Chloe.

"All of them?"

"Yes, Billy," said Stanley.

"Even the iPads?"

"All of them, Billy," Chloe reiterated.

Billy suddenly went pale. His bottom lip trembled.

"Is everything okay, Billy?" Chloe asked, suddenly concerned by Billy's dramatic reaction to the news.

"What about Billy 2000 and Billy 2000 Junior?" he murmured.

"Gone too, I'm afraid," confirmed Stanley.

Billy looked devastated. Stanley was sure that he could see tears welling up in his eyes, and looked at Chloe, unsure as to how to handle this. Billy slowly lowered his head to the desk. He was so upset by the news that his beloved desktop computer and tablet had been stolen that he started reading the textbook and doing the work that Mrs Jeeraz had set. He didn't say a word for the rest of the lesson.

The rest of the day drifted by as usual and the entertainment that had greeted the pupils on their arrival first thing that morning was soon forgotten by most. Chloe, of course, hadn't forgotten about it, and it was the first thing she mentioned when the three of them left school at the end of the day.

"Maybe we can help Constable Green to solve this crime?" she suggested.

"You only want to help him because you fancy him, Chloe," Billy blurted out.

Chloe brushed his jibe aside without denying it. "We wouldn't have to do boring business studies," she continued, "and you might be able to get the Billy 2000s back."

Suddenly, Billy was interested. Chloe had pressed the right buttons as far as he was concerned.

Stanley wasn't so sure. "Wouldn't we be best leaving this to the experts and letting the police get on with it?"

"Constable Green gave us his card and is obviously looking for help from the local community. It would be better than sitting around doing nothing. I can't do my community film about what's happening to the school until we get a tablet to do it on. There might even be a reward."

"Now you're talking!" cried Billy in excitement.

"Come on, Stanley, let's be detectives. Luckily, I've been trained in this sort of thing by the government, so if you need any help then just let me know. And I know just the place where we can start planning all this."

"Where would that be, Billy?" Stanley asked in a mocking tone.

"My HQ, of course, at my house," Billy revealed eagerly.

"You mean your garage?" probed Chloe.

"Exactly, Chloe."

Billy and Chloe both turned to Stanley. Their smiles and pleading eyes were ganging up on him. There was a sigh of dying resistance as he gave in to their demands.

"That's agreed, then," Chloe declared. "We go home, get changed, grab something to eat and then meet at Billy's garage – I mean headquarters – at 1800 hours."

"Great, see you later, team." Billy hurled his rucksack over his shoulder and sped off like a dog let off a lead.

"What exactly are we going to do at Billy's?" Stanley queried.

Chloe wasn't sure. "I haven't got that far yet, Stan. We need to get our thinking caps on."

Chapter Nineteen

SIDNEY RAIN SPENT the morning in bed. He didn't even go downstairs to make a cup of tea, even though it had been a few hours since Stanley had kindly grabbed him one before he trooped off to school. He wasn't exactly sure why he was lying in bed. It could be because his back ached a bit, although nowhere near as much as he had pretended to Stanley. After all, he needed a reason to give his son as to why he wasn't going to work that day. Sure, he would tell him in good time that he was unemployed and there wasn't much money in the household kitty, but that could wait. He didn't fancy telling him just yet. He didn't want to tell anybody yet, and so there was another reason for staying in the house again all day.

Additionally, he had taken a bang on the head last night after his fall from the wall near Shigbeth School. Everybody knows that you should be careful after a knock to the head and it is best to monitor the situation for a while before resuming normal duties; he'd seen that on the telly. What made it worse was that he still couldn't remember what he was doing climbing up the wall in the first place. Yes, he'd been out patrolling as the Raven but that was all he could remember. Perhaps he should get checked out by a doctor or go to A&E at the hospital to see if he had brain damage or something? No – best to stay in bed and rest, he decided. He had no van and so he would only have to walk there and back or catch the bus; getting a taxi would be too expensive for somebody with no income coming in.

However, underneath all the blows to his back and his skull, there was a root cause for Sid opting to just lounge in bed staring at the four walls of his bedroom. The stark truth of the matter was that he had nothing to do any more. He had lost his job. He had nothing to get up for. Last night, he had been full of renewed energy and fight, vowing to burst into the job centre and find something better than any job that Nigel Greenstock could ever offer him. He'd even instilled hope in his good friend Terry Funk that tomorrow would be better than today. Then he'd kitted himself out proudly as the Raven and strode out with head held high, eager to keep the citizens of Shigbeth safe from harm. This morning, he had woken up and all that optimism and spirit had gone. Now, he felt flat and hopeless again, like a balloon with the air escaped.

It was, however, deathly boring lying in bed, and so towards midday, Sidney decided to wrap his dressing gown around himself and go on a little adventure down to the kitchen. He made himself a cup of tea and opened a tin of tomato soup that he discovered in a rather barren cupboard. He made a quick mental note that he would have to go shopping at some point that afternoon or he and Stanley would soon starve to death. It was while he was spooning the hot, red soup into his mouth that there was a knock at the front door. Sidney ignored it at first, hoping it would go away, but then there came another set of knocks, then a pause and then more banging. Sidney placed his bowl and spoon down on the side and peered around the kitchen door into the hall and towards the front door.

The letter box flapped open and a voice called, "Sidney, are you in?"

It was Terry Funk. They'd arranged to go to the job centre today. Sidney had hoped that Terry might forget, or perhaps would have been willing to go by himself. In spite of his speech last night about seizing the day, he wasn't really in the mood for leaving the house, let alone beginning the search for work. Maybe he should just ignore him and continue to hide, but Terry wasn't giving in easily.

"Come on, Sid, answer the door."

The letter box flapped shut again. Sidney took two steps forward, and then retreated back around the corner into the kitchen. Then he moved out into the hall and reluctantly began to make his way towards the commotion at the front door. He called out the first thing that came into his head.

"Hold on a minute, I've not got any pants on," he claimed.

The letter box opened again and Terry's voice projected through the silver opening. "I thought we were going down the job centre today to find work?" he exclaimed.

Sidney hesitated for a moment. "I've not been well, Terry, lad. Sorry. I've hurt my back and must have eaten something that disagreed with me. I've been on the toilet most of the morning. I'm a couple of bags of sugar lighter than I was first thing."

There was a pause as, on the other side of the door, Terry digested this stark confession. The flap of the letter box poked up again. "But you promised, Sidney."

Sidney crouched down and lifted the flap with his index finger so he could speak through the gap too. "I can't help it if I've got the trots, Terry. It would be a bit embarrassing looking for a job and me having to leave every minute because I needed the bog."

"You said you'd come with me, though," begged Terry. He kept the flap up in anticipation of a reply.

"I know, Terry, lad, but we could go tomorrow instead. I might be better by then. Think it might be one of those twenty-four-hour stomach bugs."

"It might be too late by then. All the jobs might have gone. It's not just you and me that have been fired, Sid. Sounds like they are replacing the whole office since Greenstock took over."

"There's not a lot I can do. I'm practically chained to the toilet."

"Are you going to open the door, Sidney?" Terry requested with his face parallel to Sidney's on the other side of the door.

"I can't really, no. I'm in a right state to be honest. I've only just put me pants back on."

Terry didn't answer. Sidney felt the silence and peered through the letter box. Terry had moved away from the front door and was slowly edging his way down the path to the garden gate. He looked miserable and dejected. Sidney felt very guilty, and decided to open the front door slightly so that he could at least poke his head out and see his friend.

Terry turned back to face him. His cardigan hugged his upper body and the jet of brown hair across his forehead dangled down across his eyebrows. He needed a shave. He needed support. Sidney felt very sorry that a friend who was usually such a live wire was fast becoming an empty shell, devoid of spirit and hope.

"Look, Terry, we'll go and get new jobs tomorrow, mate," he shouted.

Terry's face did not light up. He looked as though he didn't believe the assurance that had just been given. He looked down at the gravel path and resumed his trudge away from the house. Realising he wasn't getting through to him, Sidney widened the door a little bit more, revealing his pyjamas to the world.

"Don't go, Terry. Not like this," he pleaded.

Terry paused for a moment and, encouraged by this, Sidney continued his plea.

"Tell you what, let's meet tonight for a drink," he proposed.

"But you aren't feeling very well."

"Yes, I know, but I might be better by then and getting out might do me good. We could talk strategy for when we go to the job centre. We could write down all our skills and qualifications and practise interviews on each other," Sidney urged, his face animated.

There was a glimmer of a smile on Terry's face. He'd halted his progress towards the gate.

"Let's say seven o'clock in the Rose and Crown," Sidney proposed.

Terry mulled the offer over for a moment before volunteering a response. "I suppose I could meet you for a drink."

"That's my boy." Sidney grinned, momentarily forgetting that he was supposed to be pretending that he was ill.

"Seven o'clock, you say?"

"Seven o'clock," repeated Sidney.

"At the Rose and Crown?"

"The very same," confirmed Sidney.

"I'll see you there then," agreed Terry. He smiled broadly and his body straightened.

"See you there, my old friend."

Sidney closed the door just as Terry closed the gate behind him. The house was silent again. The sun was shining through the clouds outside.

"About time I got dressed," he thought out loud.

Chapter Twenty

THE FIRST THING he did was go around the house opening up the curtains and a few windows to let the house breathe again and bathe in the warm energy that the afternoon sun was generously offering. Before getting dressed, he treated himself to a hot bath with a healthy dose of emerald-green muscle therapy bath foam to soothe his aching limbs. He lay there marooned in his own private heaven with the water gently lapping against the desert island of his belly poking up out of the ocean.

Sidney breathed deeply and rifled through his thoughts. He still had no recollection of last night before he had apparently fallen off the wall and been helped up by the old man with the dog. He'd certainly climbed up the water tower and surveyed Shigbeth from on high, as was his routine, but after that nothing sprung to mind. His back did ache a touch, but then again it often had recently, particularly after chasing the shoplifting teenager a few days before. There was a lump on the back of his head, too. He rubbed at it as he lathered his hair in shampoo. Maybe he wasn't cut out for this any more? Perhaps he did need a helping hand like the old man had suggested? He needed a partner, and Terry Funk was the only person he could think of that he would dare to ask. Should he ask Terry and give up his secret at the same time? Revealing that you sometimes dressed up as a sort of costumed vigilante superhero was not the sort of thing you made a habit of letting people know, let alone the admission that you also went out around town at night dressed like that. How would Terry react? Would he laugh in his face? Would he tell others, and should Sid therefore take the risk of trusting him with this revelation?

Bubbles broke the surface of the water as he broke wind.

Without the van, he walked to the local supermarket about twenty-five minutes away. There was next to nothing in the house and he needed to get some groceries in before Stanley came home after school for his tea. Sidney checked his bank balance at the cash machine by the entrance. There wasn't a lot of money left in his account; he would have to find a new job pronto. He resolved to do this tomorrow with Terry. There could be no more excuses for lying around in bed wishing the day away.

He took his time shopping, keen to weigh up prices and ensure that what he was buying was on offer or gave exceptional value for money. Desperate times called for desperate measures. Big breakfasts were out and muesli was in, whether this disappointed both Stanley and himself or not. After checkout, he hauled his two large bags of groceries past the magazine kiosk on his way out and stopped for a quick look at the comics. He'd been a fan since he was little. As a treat his dad used to bring one home for him every Friday, and that had fast become the highlight of his week and his childhood. Naturally, the ones featuring superheroes and crime-fighters were the best. Fantastic, colourful creations of larger-than-life characters with special powers, determined to fight evil wherever it appeared; fuel for an active imagination. Sometimes, at night as the Raven, he was almost one of these special creations. Now, at this moment, he felt very ordinary and not special at all; stood in a supermarket, no different to hundreds of others struggling to carry bags of shopping rather than busying themselves tackling foul demons and criminal masterminds. As he turned to leave, he thought again about the idea of recruiting help for his night-time hobby. A few of the comics grouped together on the shelves dealt with alliances of superheroes, great names combining forces to defeat enemies, such as the X-Men, the Avengers and the Fantastic Four. In his mind, all the way home, he played out conversations in which he told Terry his secret, but none of them ended with Terry wishing to don a costume of his own and join forces. Perhaps there were others who might be interested? However,

Sidney had already concluded that Terry was his only real friend and therefore his sole option.

It had been hard work dragging the bags of shopping. It was much easier when all he had to do was sling them in the back of the van. It was gone six o'clock and there was no sign of Stanley yet. He would have to get going eventually as he was due to meet Terry at the Rose and Crown at seven. He didn't want to be late and let Terry down again. Sidney made Stanley a huge sandwich and slid it into the fridge on a plate wrapped with cling film. He wrote a message on a piece of paper and left it on the kitchen table in case Stanley returned while he was out. He planned to try and find him first to let him know, as he was most probably round at Chloe's house, or Billy's. Sidney would call at those addresses before moving on to meet Terry at the pub. Before he left the house, he put on a clean shirt and gave himself a quick splash of 'Shark Bait', his favourite aftershave, and then headed for Chloe's.

Chapter Twenty-One

SIDNEY PRESSED AND released the doorbell of Chloe Scott's home and waited politely for a response. After a short wait, the front door was opened by a woman in a fluffy pink dressing gown. Her hair was wrapped in a white towel and her toes poked out from a pair of pink slippers. It wasn't Chloe, and it certainly wasn't Stanley.

"Miss Scott?" Sidney enquired.

"Yes, dear," came the response.

"It's Sidney Rain; Stanley's dad. I was wondering if Stanley was here, you know, with Chloe?"

Chloe's mum looked him up and down and twizzled her hair with the towel while her head tilted at forty-five degrees. She feigned embarrassment at answering the door half dressed.

"Ooh, whatever must you think of me answering the door in this state? I've only just got out of the bath."

Sidney was a little embarrassed. "I'm sorry but I need to get a message to Stanley. I'm going out and I've left his tea in the fridge for him when he gets back."

"Oh, he's a lovely lad, is Stanley. Such a polite young man, a real gentleman. I can see where he gets it from now. He's a chip off the old block, and a real credit to you. You must be a fantastic dad," she enthused.

Sidney started to blush as Miss Scott's eyes crawled all over him from head to toe and back again. He wasn't really used to female attention or strangers praising him for the way he brought up his son.

"Is there a Mrs Rain?" she asked.

"No, there isn't. It's just me," he replied.

She smiled and then started nodding her head. "It's hard, isn't it, bringing a child up on your own? I know exactly what it takes with my Chloe. There's no Mr Scott, by the way."

There was an uncomfortable pause.

"Is Stanley here?" Sidney asked again.

Chloe's mum was staring at him and seemed somewhat transfixed. She blew a lock of damp hair out of her eyes. "Is who here?" she murmured.

"My Stanley; is he here with your Chloe?"

"No, neither of them is here, I'm afraid. I haven't seen either of them. I'm completely on my own. There's no one around. It's just me."

"Oh, okay then, it was worth a try. I'll try elsewhere, then." Sidney made to move away from the house and try Billy's house.

Chloe's mum stopped him. "Before you go, you

wouldn't mind doing me a favour, would you please, Mr Rain?"

"It's Sidney. Pleased to meet you, Miss Scott," he announced, offering his hand. Chloe's mum grabbed it and they shook hands.

"Pleased to meet you, Sidney, I'm Stephanie by the way." She held his hand slightly longer than was usual for a handshake. "Oh, haven't you got strong hands?" she remarked, and gave a little giggle, fluttering her eyelashes as she did.

"How can I help?" asked Sidney.

"Well, I couldn't ask you to carry that pot plant over there round to the back gate for me, could I? It's far too heavy for delicate me to manage and shouldn't be a problem for a big, strong man like you."

"No problem at all, Miss Scott – I mean Stephanie." Sidney came over all manly, walking over to the pot plant and lifting it up in one big heave.

Chloe's mum licked her lips as she watched him. "I'll just disappear for a moment and open the back gate up for you, thank you ever so much," she said, and quickly jumped behind the front door.

By the time Sidney had made it to the back gate with the heavy plant pot, Chloe's mum had already opened it and had undergone a remarkable transformation. Her hair had been brushed, she had put on a little lipstick, and had changed out of her dressing gown and into a dress. Sidney couldn't believe it was the same woman as it had all happened so quickly.

"Aren't you strong?" she noted. "Do you work out?"

Sidney rested his delivery on the floor at her feet. "I used to be in the army many moons ago," he boasted.

"Ooh, you can't half tell," Chloe's mum cooed. "Look at those muscles."

Sidney readjusted his shirt and noticed that, by moving the pot, his nice clean shirt was now streaked with soil. Miss Scott offered to help.

"Ooh, look at you, you've gone and dirtied your shirt! Why don't you take it off and I'll chuck it in the wash for you?"

"That's very kind of you, Miss Scott – I mean Stephanie – but I'm sure it will be fine." He brushed the soil off, but a black streak of dirt remained visible across his chest.

"It'll be my pleasure, Sidney, don't be shy," she said, reaching out to tug at his shirt.

"I need to get a move on and find Stanley if it's all the same, Miss Stephanie, so I'll make a move if you don't mind. Lovely to meet you," he said as he backed away from the front gate.

"Bye, Sidney Rain," she called as he hurried down the drive. "We'll meet again I expect."

Sidney felt her eyes burn into his back as he made his exit. Once out of the road, he even checked over his shoulder to make sure she wasn't chasing him. It was usually about ten minutes' walk from the Scott to the Bathurst residence. Sidney was there in five.

Chapter Twenty-Two

"COME INTO MY office," Billy said, and led Stanley and Chloe to the back of his mum and dad's garage. It wasn't the first time that Billy had invited them into his 'office', as he put it. A wooden door led inside to where Billy switched on a light. Suddenly, they were again surrounded by the amazing and slightly strange world of Billy Bathurst. There was a workbench and a chair, behind which was a wall festooned with posters of spacecraft and planets, drawings of aliens and superheroes, and newspaper cuttings. The garage was cluttered with toys and model trains and planes, and there were mobiles hanging from wires on the ceiling and displays of planets in a multitude of colours. It was almost like they had stepped into Billy's head; his vivid imagination made real.

"Make yourselves at home," he said, his face glowing with pride. It was hard to find a place to sit down amidst all the junk and paraphernalia. As there was only a single chair, Stanley pulled up a wooden box from the corner of the room and he and Chloe perched their bottoms on either end of it. Billy pulled up his chair opposite them on the other side of the workbench like he was a chairman of the board.

Chloe spoke first. "Right, boys, the idea of this meeting is to come up with some ideas on how we can go about helping PC Green find the thieves who stole our computers from school."

Billy chimed his agreement with the agenda. "Yes, I definitely think we should do something about finding the computers. I want my Billy 2000 family back." He grabbed a pencil and a bit of rough paper and started writing. "How do you spell 'meeting'?"

"M… E… A… T… I… N," volunteered Stanley sneeringly. Billy wrote the incorrect spelling down without hesitation, his tongue pushing into his cheek as he concentrated.

"And we also need to talk about what we can do to let people know that what is happening to our school is wrong," continued Chloe.

Billy gave up writing for a moment. He was an ideas man, not a pen-pusher. "Right, what've we got, team? Hit me!" Stanley quickly thought about punching him in the face and sending him flying across the garage.

"Well, for starters," responded Chloe, "we could go and see Charlie – I mean Constable Green – and find out what he knows about the theft. Were there any sightings or witnesses? Does he know when the theft happened?"

"It happened last night," chirped Billy.

"Yes, I realise that, Billy, but what time during the night? Was it during the evening in daylight, or was it in the dead of night when it was pitch-black? We should also check if the police know how the computers were taken. How many criminals were there? Have there been any other similar thefts reported recently?"

"So, we visit the police station and chat with PC Green, then?" interrupted Stanley.

"Yes, Stan," agreed Chloe, "I reckon we need more information and details first, and then we can proceed from there. How about you and I go there after school tomorrow?"

Billy and Stanley nodded their approval. Billy wrote down the words *police station visit* on his sheet of paper and put a giant tick next to them.

"That's agreed, then," confirmed Chloe. "Any other thoughts?"

"I'd like to do a stake-out," volunteered Billy. "Detectives do it all the time on the American cop shows. It'd be brilliant. They sit in cars waiting for the criminals to show and eat snacks!"

"We haven't got a car, Billy," Stanley pointed out.

"No, but we could keep watch outside of school in case there are more thefts. There are plenty of places to hide."

Stanley was less than impressed. "Are you seriously suggesting that we stay up all night in all weathers, hanging around school in case the thieves decide to return?"

Chloe didn't answer. She joined Billy in staring at Stanley.

"Yeah, come on, it will be fun," Billy insisted.

"The last thing I want to do is spend more time at school. I spend all day there as it is without spending all night there as well," Stanley reasoned.

Billy was undeterred and was rather animated about his plans for a stake-out. "We could take biscuits and drinks and things, and stay up all night keeping watch and telling each other ghost stories."

Stanley's concerns about Billy's ideas were clearly not registering with him. He turned to Chloe in a plea for sanity to prevail. "There is very little chance that the thieves will return to the scene of their crime," he argued.

Chloe gave him no help. "That may be the case, Stan, but it does sound like it could be fun."

Billy put his palms together as if in prayer. "Go on, Stanley, let's do it," he encouraged.

"I don't know, Billy; it doesn't really make a lot of sense."

Billy changed his approach. "Is it because you are scared about sneaking out at night?"

Stanley looked at Chloe for support. She looked back at him inquisitively, waiting for his response to the charge.

"No, it's not that I'm scared. I've done it before, loads of times." Stanley was very aware that he didn't want Chloe to think less of him.

"Great, that's agreed then," announced Billy, writing the words *steak out* on his list and granting the plan another massive tick of approval. "I can bring my army night-vision goggles as well."

"Maybe tomorrow night after we've got the latest information at the police station?" added Chloe. She and Billy looked at Stanley, awaiting final approval.

"Go on then, I suppose it could be a bit of a laugh," he agreed.

"Hopefully, we might bump into the Raven while we're out and about," Billy added, nodding at a newspaper cutting attached to the wall.

"We've more chance of bumping into Harry Potter" muttered Stanley caustically.

Billy dropped his pencil on the table in protest. "I've seen him for myself, Stan, so I know he's real. If you doubt me, just look at the drawings of him over there." He pointed to a group of sketches on the wall of a shadowy figure with a cloak and the face of a bird.

"Drawing something isn't proof that it exists, Billy. People draw pictures of all sorts of things from their imaginations; they aren't real just because you've dreamt them up, you know."

Billy wasn't backing down. He raised himself from his chair. "I've seen him for myself, and so have others.

There's a newspaper cutting of a report that he was seen as well, not just by me."

He was correct in that, a couple of years back, there had been a flurry of interest after a couple of apparent sightings. The local paper had taken a fleeting interest until those in Shigbeth who even bothered to read it largely dismissed the story as a hoax or the mad ramblings of a drunk coming home from the pub late at night after six or seven pints of beer too many.

"That was just some nutter in a bin liner," concluded Stanley.

"It was a cloak and he was real," stated Billy adamantly.

Chloe decided to calm things down before it all became too heated. "Now then you two, let's focus on the job in hand and the meeting, please."

Billy sat down again and retrieved the pencil from the workbench. Stanley unfolded himself and leant back on the wooden box next to Chloe.

"As well as the business with the theft of the computers, I also think that we should start tackling the problem of our school being taken over by that awful Greenstock character," Chloe said.

Billy and Stanley, having calmed down, nodded their agreement.

"I'm going to draw up a petition for students and parents to sign to register their displeasure at what is happening to Shigbeth School. It's being turned into a business acting in the interests of its new owner and not those that really matter: the students. We've had basketball club cancelled and our uniform is being changed without consultation. Who's going to help me get this petition organised?"

Stanley was the first to offer his support, but not without reservation. "I'll help you do it, Chloe, but I'm not so sure it will make any difference."

"Well that's not the right sort of attitude, Stanley Rain. Why won't it make a difference?" asserted Chloe, looking mighty annoyed that someone had dared to frown upon her idea.

"It's just that the school takeover has already been agreed. It's got this far, so somebody somewhere who's more important than us has said that it's okay."

Chloe's eyes narrowed. "Who is more important at Shigbeth School than the students, Stanley?"

Stanley looked at Billy for support, but he was quite enjoying Stanley's current predicament, squirming as Chloe pressed him.

"Well, no one really, but I just don't think the world works like that. When all's said and done, I don't think that we have much say in anything. Maybe it's because we are just kids and no one really cares much for what we think," Stanley replied.

"Well, maybe that's wrong and maybe it ought to change," railed Chloe. "Nobody ever changed the world by sitting on their backside and giving in. I'm going to write to our MP as well and ask her what she thinks about what is going on under her nose at the local school."

"Great idea, Chloe," said Billy, smiling at Stanley as he said it.

"That's agreed then," confirmed Chloe. "Stanley and I will start working on the petition and the letter to our MP. Billy, you can start making plans for the stake-out tomorrow night in terms of equipment. Stanley and I will go to the police station straight after school tomorrow to see what PC Green has to offer on the theft."

The two boys nodded their approval. Stanley started looking around the garage for more paper. Billy went looking for his army-issue night-vision goggles.

Chapter Twenty-Three

SIDNEY WAS STILL checking that he hadn't been followed by Chloe's mum as he rapped at the front door of the Bathurst residence. Surely, Stanley would be here since he wasn't at Chloe's house? Billy's house was quite a big detached place with a slope leading up to a big blue front door with a frosted panel of glass in the centre. Sidney heard footsteps from beyond it and there was a blur of colour through the glass as the door leaned outwards on opening. A tall man with curly grey hair poked his head around the door.

"Is Stanley there?" asked Sidney.

The curly-haired door opener looked Sidney up and down and then gestured for him to enter, no word of greeting passing from his lips. Sidney found himself in a hallway with a set of sweeping stairs arrowing their way towards the ceiling on his right-hand side. The decor seemed tired and old and the walls were peppered with framed photographs of the family in awkward poses.

Eager to break the silence, Sidney fished for introductions. He held his hand out. "I'm Sidney Rain, Stanley's dad."

Billy's dad responded, offering a hand of friendship in return. "Bobby Bathurst," he said, "Billy's dad." Both of them squeezed a little harder with their handshakes and held on for a touch longer than usual to lay down a marker of their strength and manliness. When they'd finished, it became obvious that Bobby had noticed the dark soil stain that was streaked across Sidney's shirt.

"Have you been round the Scotts' house?" Bobby enquired.

Sidney was confused. How did he know? "Yes, just now," he admitted. He was about to ask what had given it away when a woman's piercing voice shouted down from upstairs.

"Who is it?" she screamed.

Bobby looked embarrassed and all his apparent manliness seemed to shrivel up into a little ball. "It's nothing, dear, it's just Stanley's dad," he called back up the stairs.

"Well, tell him to get lost," came the retort from on high.

Both Sidney and Bobby were a little taken aback by this response.

"No, my little wallflower, its Stanley's dad, Sidney," Bobby reiterated.

This time there was no response and the two dads just smiled at each other as they waited for an answer.

Sidney started taking an interest in the photographs on the wall as a distraction from the uncomfortable silence.

Bobby Bathurst whispered an apology. "Sorry about that, Sidney. I think my wife is going out to bingo in a minute."

Sidney nodded with feigned understanding.

"She gets a bit excited."

Sidney pointed at one of the photographs. It showed what must have been a younger Bobby, with short hair and stood to attention in military uniform, all crisp lines and polished buttons. "This you, Bobby? Were you in the army?"

Bobby stood proudly as if someone had snapped an order at him to stand to attention. Beneath the grey, curly hair he still cut a good figure of a man. Sidney noticed he was taller than he himself was, with thick shoulders and long legs beneath his blue sweater and black trousers.

"Yes, Sidney, I did a bit of service when I was younger," he confirmed proudly. "What about yourself?"

Sidney stood to attention and clicked his heels together. "Yes, Sir, Private Sidney Rain from the 23rd Engineering Corps. Which unit were you in?"

"I was in various units, but did a lot of time in Special Forces," he replied.

Sidney was a bit stung by that, as Special Forces were impressive; they only took the best soldiers from each army section. "Yes, I did a few sessions with Extra-Special Forces," he answered.

"I've never heard of them," queried Bobby.

"No, well, you won't have done – it was all top-secret stuff, back in the day," Sidney boasted, and gave Bobby a little wink. "Sometimes, it was so top-secret, I didn't even know I was in it."

"So you'll have done a bit of parachuting then? What height did you tend to jump from?" Bobby asked.

Sidney hesitated a bit at this, pursing his lips in concentration. "We did about a thousand feet or so."

"Blimey, is that all?" Bobby responded in surprise. "We used to free-fall from twelve thousand before we even dreamt about parachuting. I bet you must have done some long-range rifle shooting, though?"

Sidney was again on the back foot and having to come up with something impressive to match Bobby's boasts. "Yeah, I used to be able to hit a target from about five hundred feet away." He didn't really know what he was talking about, but didn't want to lose face with another dad. Sure, he'd fired a gun in basic training, but he was an engineer in the army, not a fighter. He'd never really been part of any exciting action such as the type of stuff that Billy's dad was suggesting that he had done.

"We used to hit our targets from nearer one thousand feet," claimed Bobby.

"Yeah, but I could've done that if they'd let me take my blindfold off," Sidney asserted.

Bobby was clearly confused. "Why did you practise shooting targets with a blindfold on?" he asked, looking puzzled.

"In case we had to shoot someone at night," Sidney explained.

There was a pause as the contest about which of them had been the world's greatest soldier subsided. Another shout tumbled down the stairs from Mrs Bathurst.

"Has he gone yet?"

Bobby seemed to jump as he snapped to attention yet again for his domestic sergeant major. "No, my love, we are just off to the games room to get Stanley." He gently urged Sidney back out of the front door and they headed around the side of the house to a door at the back of the garage. "We call it the games room but it's really just the garage where Billy plays and keeps some of his stuff," he explained. "He even sleeps in there sometimes."

Sidney couldn't really work out Bobby Bathurst. On one hand he seemed to have once been a proud, strong soldier, but he also seemed to shake in fright whenever he heard the voice of his wife. Also, there was the fact that he had once prided himself on his appearance. The photograph of the fresh-faced young soldier with the crew-cut hair seemed very different from the weary-eyed, curly, grey-haired man of today. Sidney knew that one thing life in the army taught you was that things should be tidy and shipshape with everything in order and in its proper place. The Bathurst household showed no signs of this. The inside of the house was poorly maintained and the garden was overgrown, with bricks and cardboard boxes shooting out of the ground rather than carefully manicured flowers and neatly trimmed bushes and stretches of lawn. The Bobby Bathurst of the past didn't seem to connect with the Bobby Bathurst of today.

Bobby opened the rusty-hinged door at the back of the garage and a shaft of light revealed Stanley, Billy and Chloe cramped around a workbench laden with bits of paper. Billy moved his arm guardedly over the sheets as though trying to hide their contents.

"Your dad is here, Stanley," announced Bobby, somewhat needlessly as they did know who each other was.

"Have you been round to my house Mr Rain?" asked Chloe.

"Yes. How did you know?" demanded Sidney.

"I can tell by your shirt. Did my mum make you move a plant pot?"

Sidney looked down at the mark on his shirt. Bobby smirked.

"She does that to all the men that call round. Did you move it from the back garden to the front?" Chloe continued.

"She asked me to move it round to the back."

"The next fella that calls round will be moving it

back round to the front then, I expect," she surmised. "Did she have any clothes on when she answered the door?"

Sidney started to confirm that she did have clothes on, but Stanley recognised the embarrassment that his dad felt and interrupted the grilling.

"Are you okay, Dad?" he asked.

"Yes, son, I'm fine. It's just, I'm going to the pub tonight and won't be back till a bit later, so I've come round to tell you that I have done a nice plate of food for you and popped it in the fridge. Make sure you get yourself to bed as usual, you know the routine."

Stanley gave a quick yes to the instructions, his cheeks flushing a little as his dad had hinted at his bedtime in front of his friends. Then his dad's plans for the evening suddenly struck him. "You're going to the pub? You were feeling ill this morning. That's why you didn't go into work."

Sidney squirmed a little, realising that Stanley might be on to him. "No, son, that was just backache. I'm feeling much better now and I'll be back in work tomorrow."

"Do you like my office, Mr Rain?" Billy blurted out.

Sidney's eyes trawled around the garage, taking in the planets hovering above his head, suspended by coat-hanger wire from the ceiling, and the walls decorated with pictures and bits of card and newspaper. One section particularly caught his interest. It was an area covered in snippets harvested from the front pages of comics; various posing superheroes in colourful costumes. Pencil sketches, presumably by Billy, were pinned between them.

"Yes, you seem to be quite an artist, Billy. I like all the superheroes too. I used to read a lot of stuff like this when I was younger. Which one is your favourite?"

Billy jumped up from his chair over to a drawing that he had done. "This one's my favourite," he asserted proudly.

"Which one's that?" asked Sidney.

"It's the Raven," he replied.

For a split second, Sidney didn't know what to say or where to look.

"He's not real, Billy," interrupted Stanley.

"Yes he is. I've seen him."

Bobby turned to Sidney. "He's got a very active imagination, has my boy."

"He is real, Dad, he even waved at me one time, and others have met him. He's been in the newspaper and he's captured criminals and helped the police before, too. He's my hero." Billy pointed to a news story cut from the *Shigbeth Gazette* that was also pinned to the wall.

Sidney tried hard not to display any recognition on his face, owing to the fact that he had exactly the same article in his bedside drawer at home. He also tried valiantly not to give away that he was bursting with pride that his alter ego was the idol of a twelve-year- old boy.

Fortunately, everyone was interrupted by a shout from the garden. It was Mrs Bathurst, informing them that she was off out to bingo for the evening. Sidney was sure that Bobby cowered when he heard her shriek. Her leaving was a cue for everyone to continue with their business, so the two fathers left their sons with Chloe to carry on with whatever it was they were up to tucked away in the confines of the games-room-cum-office-cum-garage.

"So you're at work tomorrow then, Sidney. What do you do for a living now that you're not away fighting for Queen and Country?" asked Bobby as the men walked from the garage to the front garden.

Having lost his job only a few days ago, Sidney was a touch hesitant and unsure as to what his answer might be. He also didn't want to lose face with Bobby, who probably had a much more successful job now to go with his clearly much more glamorous former life as a soldier.

"Well, to tell you the truth I didn't really have backache today and I'm not going to work tomorrow either. I used to be a van driver, for years until this week and then I kind of got made redundant," Sidney revealed. It was a far more honest answer than he had expected to give, but it just seemed to fall from his lips that way.

Bobby stopped walking. "Not easy, is it? It happens to the best of us."

"You mean you haven't a job either?"

"It's been a few months now," Bobby confessed. "Well, I've had a few placements and done bits of training and different courses, but nothing concrete as yet, nothing permanent anyway."

"Sorry, Bobby, I didn't realise. You don't seem the sort of bloke to be out of work."

"Well, I could very easily say the same about you, Sidney. We've both got skills; I mean, I'm a driver too, of lorries, but I can't seem to find anything that sticks at the moment; gets a bit hard to take sometimes. The wife thinks I'm useless, of course, and fit for the knacker's yard. Then again, it's her wage that's currently paying the mortgage and putting food on the table."

"Does Billy know?" asked Sidney, nodding towards the garage.

"I haven't found a way of telling him yet, but I think he's noticed that I'm home a lot more than usual and he will have heard how the wife has been screaming at me more and more. I'm guessing that Stanley doesn't know either?"

Sidney shook his head. "Too early for me, can't do it. I don't want him thinking that his old man isn't wanted by anyone. Last thing you want is for your son to realise that you're a bit of a failure. I rather like the illusion that I'm not; that's taken years of work to build up."

"Don't give up yet, Sid, it's only been a couple of days. Something will show up."

"It hasn't for you yet, Bob, so maybe it won't for me either."

The two of them stood there and smiled, even though by all accounts there wasn't much to be cheery about. Then Sidney had an idea.

"Look, why don't you come down to the Rose and Crown with me for a drink? I'm meeting my friend Terry, he's a great laugh usually but he's been down in the dumps recently because he got laid off only yesterday from the same company as I did."

Bobby wasn't keen, and his nose wrinkled in response. "I can't really, especially if the wife finds out."

"Who's going to tell her? It doesn't seem fair that she's allowed to go out gallivanting at the bingo while you're stuck in. While the mice are away, the cat will play. We won't be long, just a quick pint, that's all," urged Sidney.

"Well, I suppose I could have a quick drink," Bobby accepted.

"No 'suppose' about it, mate! Come on, it will do you good. We could talk about the old days, and Terry is an absolute legend."

"Okay, you've sold it to me. I'll just go and let Billy know that I'm nipping down the shops or something. I should be with you in ten minutes or so after I've got changed."

"Brilliant, Bobby. See you later then," said Sidney as he watched Bobby venture back to the garage to tell his son. He wondered whether he should reveal his secret to Bobby as well as Terry. After all, sometimes you need help from someone else; some of the comics he'd seen in the supermarket had taught him that much. One more recruit and they could be the Fantastic Four.

Chapter Twenty-Four

DURING THE WALK to the pub, Sidney's brain rattled through scenarios in which he revealed his secret and invited his friends to join him on his twilight escapades. Thinking about coming clean made his stomach spin like a washing machine. One minute he was going to do it; his heart urging him to share this exciting idea with the others. However, a minute later his head was in command, all logical and rational, threatening that they would only laugh at him and he would die of embarrassment.

There was no sign of Terry Funk when he strode past the wooden benches and the rainbows of flowers in tubs at the entrance to the Rose and Crown public house, but then again he was a little early. He had let Terry down earlier in the day by not joining him for the visit to the job centre, but surely Terry would meet with him tonight after what was said across his front doorstep this afternoon? The pub was busy, with people partaking in post-work drinks and the weather turning nicely bright and warm for a change. Sidney made his way to the bar where the landlord stood polishing pint glasses with a green tea towel. He had a grey beard that reminded Sid of Bobby Bathurst's hair colour, and a shiny black waistcoat that seemed to be too small and squeezed his ribcage.

"Can I interest you in one of our new real ales, Sir?" he asked.

"I'm not really into those," said Sidney. "I've never really tried one before."

"How do you know that you aren't into them, if you haven't tried one?" noted the landlord. He handed Sidney a list of all the different beers. They all seemed to have strange names and descriptions, the sort you might find on a food menu in a fancy restaurant.

He chose one because he liked the name. "Go on then, I'll try a pint of Badger's Revenge, please."

"Good choice, Sir," said the landlord, who proceeded to drain the contents of a silver tube into a glass and then hand it over in exchange for a five-pound note. The contents of the glass swirled around in silvery clouds before settling into a liquid with the colour of soil. Sidney received his change and gave the strange brew a slurp.

"Very nice," he acknowledged.

"Nothing ventured, nothing gained," said the landlord, fixing him in his gaze.

"Nothing ventured, nothing gained," repeated Sidney.

He had just sat down in the evening sunshine on a wooden bench by the side of the car park when he spotted Bobby. His grey curly hair was instantly recognisable. He'd tidied himself up a bit too; he'd popped on a clean shirt, which made Sidney think about the mess his was in after meeting Stephanie Scott.

"Sidney," Bobby greeted him.

"Bobby," said Sidney.

"Do you want a drink?" Bobby asked, which seemed like a strange question because there was one on the table right in front of Sidney.

"No thanks, Bob, I've already got one," he replied, pointing at the drink sitting in front of him just in case Bobby hadn't noticed it. "They've got some real ale on tonight. Ask the barman if you can see the list when you go in. I've got Badger's Revenge."

Bobby seemed a little confused, but headed off inside the pub. He came back a few minutes later with a pint of Old Granny's Crankshaft.

"I haven't got too long, Sid. If I don't get back before the wife gets home from bingo I'm a dead man walking."

"I wouldn't worry, Bob. It won't be a late night for me either. I can't drink more than a couple of pints these days before falling asleep, and I've got to get back for Stanley anyway."

"So where's your friend then?" asked Bobby, pulling up a chair round the table.

"Terry should be here any moment. He's a top

bloke, he is. After we've finished here, he'll probably head out into town and go clubbing or something, even though he's in the same boat as us. We're heading down the job centre tomorrow morning. You can join us if you want."

"Aye, I might just do that – as long as the missus doesn't find out I've been out to the pub and I'm still alive."

Bobby nearly spat out his next mouthful of beer as he saw a strange character arrive at the entrance to the pub car park. The man had a chequered cardigan on, with grey, flared trousers flapping against his white trainers. Strands of mousy brown hair also flapped across his forehead and threatened to cover the thick-rimmed lenses of his spectacles, rendering him blind. Bobby nudged Sidney with his elbow, causing him to spill a little of his beer on the table. "Look at the state of him."

"Terry!" shouted Sidney across the car park as he leapt up from his seat to get the man's attention.

"Terry?" muttered Bobby in surprise.

"Bobby Bathurst, meet Terry Funk," announced Sidney.

Terry took off his spectacles and wiped them on his cardigan before offering his hand to Bobby. Bobby tried to hide his surprise and confusion with a polite smile and a firm handshake.

"Go and get yourself a drink, Terry, lad," urged Sidney. "There's a great range of beers on from all over the world. Bob and I are working our way down the list."

Five minutes later, Terry returned from inside the pub with a Black Parrot.

As the evening progressed, the sun began to go down and the numbers of people in the pub ebbed and flowed. The three of them were soon the only group sat outside at the wooden tables as the temperature cooled and darkness started to settle. It was later than they realised, and they had consumed more drinks than they had originally envisaged doing. In terms of Sidney getting home to Stanley and Bobby getting home before his curfew, both were sailing a little close to the wind. And if Terry was the sort of guy who was keen to get to the nightclubs and discotheques as they opened, then he too would soon have to get a move on. The truth was, however, that they were enjoying themselves a little too much to leave just yet. They had discussed their plans for getting work as soon as possible, and the pressures that their new-found unemployment put upon them and their families. They spent time tasting each other's beers and trying to judge which of them was the best, with a brew labelled Dragon's Breath narrowly defeating Uncle Growler. And as the night drew to a close, Sidney found that he was becoming increasingly relaxed and less concerned about what his friends would think of him even if he did, as he had considered earlier, reveal that he was the Raven. He knew that they would all have to go soon and the opportunity would be lost, and so headed for the toilets to steel himself before making his announcement. He couldn't continue his adventures as the Raven on his own any more. The past few days had shown him that very clearly. However, once again he was teetering on the brink of not saying anything for fear of how they would react. It would be easier to forget about it and just let his revelation lie.

As he passed the bar on his way back, the waist-coated landlord with the silver beard caught his attention.

"Fancy a final drink, Sir, before we start to shut up shop?" he asked.

"No thanks," said Sidney.

"No worries, Sir. I'm glad you enjoyed trying something different and taking a chance."

"Nothing ventured, nothing gained." The words from earlier just seemed to jump from Sidney's mouth before he could close his lips tight to stop them.

As those words tumbled into the air, Sidney realised that, like it or not, he had made a decision. This was his moment and it was written in his stars. He was going to tell them right now. He completely forgot about the barman and headed back to his friends before he lost his nerve.

"I've got something to tell you, and I realise that you might not believe what I am about to say and you might just laugh at me, but I'm going to tell you it anyway."

Terry put down his nearly finished pint. Bobby raised his to his lips. Sidney took a deep breath and went for it.

"You know that guy in the local paper, who went around town at night dressed like a superhero?" he asked.

"You mean that fruit cake in the bin liner that my Billy was mumbling about tonight?" answered Bobby.

Terry just looked puzzled. "Not really, no."

Sidney closed his eyes for a moment and offered a silent prayer to the gods. "Well, that was me."

Bobby sent a fountain of Orion's Belt, rather appropriately, into the night sky before coughing uncontrollably. Clearly, the news had sent his beer 'down the wrong way'. Terry stood up and started to pat Bobby on the back in case he was choking to death. As he recovered his posture, Bobby began to laugh.

"That's excellent, Sid, you had us going there for a moment. You're the guy in the newspaper clipping. Brilliant," chortled Bobby. As he continued to laugh, he gradually began to notice that he was the only one laughing. Terry was shooting a deadpan look at Sidney, whose face and eyes were awash with honesty.

"It's true, isn't it?" asked Terry.

"I've never been more serious," confirmed Sidney.

"You're kidding?" said Bobby, now fully recovered from his coughing fit and burst of laughter.

"I swear on Stanley's life," continued Sidney, "I'm the Raven."

"Blinking Nora," exclaimed Bobby.

Bobby and Terry grabbed hold of their glasses to steady themselves after the shock. For Sidney, the feeling wasn't one of shock. It was more a sense of huge relief, like a heavy weight had suddenly dropped from his shoulders. He felt ten years younger in an instant. He also felt proud.

"You're the guy in the newspaper cutting; the one that Billy does sketches of and pins to the wall in the garage," said Bobby.

"The very same," admitted Sidney.

"Why?" enquired Terry.

Sidney looked him straight in the eye. "Why not?" he responded. He took a final sip of his beer and slowly placed it down in front of him. "I don't always sleep well at night, and so several years ago I started going out late at night for walks. Seemed to be good exercise – you know, a bit of fresh air, peace and quiet. No one's really around at that time; the world's a very different place, very peaceful. Occasionally you hear things, though, and sometimes see things too. One night I saw a guy getting beaten up in an alleyway and I thought about helping but my feet just froze to the spot. Maybe it's because I didn't want to get hurt or didn't want anybody asking me what I was doing out at night; I don't really know. But over time, I saw other things and I just wanted to help, that's all. So I dressed more appropriately and eventually started to develop a disguise, and then a sort of character started to take shape, and before I knew it I had even given myself a name. And because it wasn't me, because it was someone stronger and better than me, I became more confident and started to get involved if I saw things. I'm sort of addicted to it, I suppose."

"Blinking Nora," interjected Bobby again.

Sidney continued with his explanation. "I guess I always wanted to be a sort of superhero. I used to read a lot of comics when I was a kid, a bit like your Billy. I suppose I didn't want to be me, all ordinary, vulnerable and afraid. I wanted to be like them, kind of special."

"So why are you telling us this now, Sidney?" asked Terry.

"I want you to join me," Sidney replied.

Bobby was flabbergasted and shouted, "You want me to run around town wrapped in a bin liner, looking through people's back windows?"

"You don't have to wrap yourself in anything, Bobby. You just become whatever character you want to be."

"Oh, I'll be Spider-Man then, because I've always been able to shoot webs out of my wrists," snorted Bobby.

"I'll help," announced Terry.

Bobby laughed. "What, I suppose you're going to be Captain Cardigan, are you?"

"There's no need to get personal, Bobby. I might well wear cardigans but at least I don't look like someone's left a bird's nest on my head,"Terry retorted. Bobby didn't seem to have a comeback for that one.

"Thanks, Terry. I can't believe it. You're a true friend and gent." Before he knew it, a beaming Sidney was giving Terry a big hug. "Come on, Bobby, we could do with your help. After all, you've got the physique and all that experience in the Special Forces could come in very useful. You seem like a guy who can handle himself in a scrap."

"No thanks, I'd have to be crazy to do this," Bobby responded.

Sidney put his hand on Bobby's shoulder. "Of course I understand if you say no and need a bit of time to think it over, especially if you're scared of your wife finding out."

"I'm not scared of my wife finding out." Bobby jerked away, affronted by the accusation that he was afraid of his 'other half'.

Sidney and Terry looked at each other, evidently disbelieving Bobby's proclamation.

"I am the boss in my house," Bobby insisted. "I don't need her permission for anything I get up to."

"No, but you'd best get back soon before she returns from bingo, otherwise you're in trouble, Bobby, lad," warned Terry.

Bobby was clearly stung by the allegation against his manliness. He folded his arms and sat back in his chair for a moment. "Right, I'm in for once and only once."

"Brilliant," said Sidney, genuinely thrilled and very much surprised at the affirmations from his friends that they were willing to give it a go.

"When?" asked Terry.

Sidney thought for a moment. "How about we all meet at the job centre tomorrow morning at ten, then come here for a quick drink so we can make plans? Then we go out as a group for the first time late tomorrow night."

"What do we do when we go out?" asked Terry.

"You leave that to me, Terry, lad, I'm an old hand at this, been doing it for years," replied Sidney.

"And I've done camouflage stuff in the army," added Bobby.

"What do we wear?" asked Terry.

"That's down to you, mate. You need to find some sort of character like I did and dress accordingly. Just go with whatever springs to mind," advised Sidney. "It'll just suddenly come to you like it did with me."

"How do we sneak out at night?" asked Bobby.

"It's no problem for me as I live on my own," said Terry.

"Yeah, that's all right for you, Terry, but what about my wife and Billy? How am I going to get out of the house without them knowing?"

"Thought you ruled the roost at your place, Bobby? Why don't you just tell them you're going out?" suggested Terry.

The three paused as different thoughts and ideas

raced through their heads. Sidney broke the silence.

"Before we go tonight, we need to make a promise about what we have just decided. I propose we take a sort of vow of allegiance; a guarantee that we will do this and follow through on what we have said. I have faith that both you guys will show up as planned tomorrow evening, but it's very easy to have second thoughts and back out of things in the cold light of day. I've been brave enough to reveal my secret tonight. I want you to match that and be courageous enough to act on your word."

He grabbed a beer mat and tore it into three pieces. "If you take a piece of this beer mat, then it is a solemn vow that we do this tomorrow night. You take the piece with you tonight and it acts as a reminder of what we promised here."

Sidney placed the divided beer mat on the table and then retrieved his piece. Terry glanced at him, and then at Bobby. He twitched his nose and his spectacles jiggled. He took the second piece. Bobby hesitated for a moment, placed his hand on the table and looked at the others.

"I must be barking mad," he said before picking up his piece and making his vow. "Blinking Nora," he added, shaking his head in disbelief at what he had just signed up for.

Chapter Twenty-Five

THE FOLLOWING AFTERNOON, Stanley and Chloe made good on their plan to visit the police station and try to get more information about the theft of the computers from PC Green; after all, he had given them his card and told them to come and see him if they had any information or had heard about anything untoward. Granted, they didn't really have anything to offer him, other than their help of course. Chloe was determined to press ahead with what was fast becoming a mission to bring to justice whoever had done this, and at the same time start fighting back against the plans for Greenstock Academy. Stanley was more reticent and perhaps realistic about their chances of success on both counts. He seriously doubted that the computers would ever be found and the criminals revealed. He also felt that the takeover of the school, along with the new uses of its facilities, new motto and new uniform, was already set in stone. This could all be an incredible waste of time, he mused. In spite of this, he was keen to support his best friend in whatever way he could.

The police station was a small but modern building about twenty-five minutes' walk from school. It was very quiet inside, with a long desk snaking around double doors that presumably led to the office where police officers were working. A line of chairs stood beside the front entrance; presumably this was the area put aside for visitors to wait in. The walls were thick with posters warning citizens of Shigbeth to be on their guard about a range of potential crimes from identity theft to dangerous dogs. It reminded Stanley a little bit of the walls in Billy's 'office'. Chloe waited at the desk for service while Stanley had a read through the leaflets of information scattered about a small table by the chairs. Eventually, a policewoman in the usual black uniform appeared from behind the doors. She seemed to file whatever pieces of paper she was carrying before turning her attention to Chloe.

"And how might I be able to help you, young lady?"

"I'm looking for Constable Green," Chloe stated, before ferreting around in her pocket for something. "He gave us his card and said that we could come and talk to him."

The policewoman screwed her eyes up at the sight of the card. "And you are…?" she demanded.

"I'm Chloe Scott from Shigbeth School, and this is my friend Stanley Rain."

The police officer glanced over at Stanley. He flicked back a nervous smile.

"Okay, Chloe and Stanley, I'll go and see if he's here." She immediately turned 180 degrees and let the double doors swallow her up. A thank-you from Chloe hung in the air as she left.

"He's probably busy tuning his guitar or rehearsing for his next sell-out world tour," joked Stanley.

"Do you think Billy's found a location for the stake-out tonight?" asked Chloe.

"Oh, I get the feeling Billy's taking this far too seriously, Chloe. He's been mapping out the area around the school already. I know he's been on the internet looking at satellite photos of the area, and he even took some photographs today of possible viewing points with that hidden camera that he built inside his school lunch box."

"Let's hope he had the camera pointing the right way round this time and he's not just taken selfies," remarked Chloe.

"Wait till you see his night-vision goggles," said Stanley. "He thinks he's James Bond."

PC Charlie Green emerged from the doors and seemed pleasantly surprised that Chloe and Stanley had visited him. "Chloe!" he exclaimed. "And…?" He'd clearly not remembered Stanley's name, and so Chloe had to finish his sentence for him. "What are you two doing here, then?"

"Hi, Constable Green. Well, the truth is we

just wanted to see how things are going with the investigation into the theft of the computers from school yesterday," said Chloe. "We want to help in any way we can."

PC Green propped his elbows on the big desk. "Well, if I'm being perfectly honest, Chloe, we haven't got very far."

"Oh," replied Chloe, who was clearly expecting more; certainly more than Stanley.

"We've got very little to go on. It really is as though the computers vanished into thin air. Nothing was broken, there's no CCTV in the school and there aren't any fingerprints. It was obviously a professional job; these guys have probably done this before – not necessarily in Shigbeth, but they know how to not leave clues."

Chloe looked puzzled and disappointed. "Were there no witnesses?"

PC Green shook his head. "Well, apart from one old chap who thought he met someone on his way back from night fishing, nobody saw or heard anything. We've drawn a complete blank so far. I'm sorry, Chloe."

"Can we help in any way?" volunteered Stanley.

"That's very good of you, young man, but not really. Look, if you find or hear anything suspicious then let me know; you've got my card with my phone number on. Tell you what, I shouldn't really do this but I'll just put my mobile number on the card for you as well in case of an emergency." Constable Green grabbed a biro and left a trail of numbers on the business card he had given Chloe. "Look, must dash," he said. "Thanks for coming down to see me, and it's great that you two are helping us out and being true citizens of Shigbeth." He smiled and shot back through the doors and out of sight.

Chloe waved her hand in farewell as the door closed. Then she turned round to face Stanley. "Do you think we should have told him about the stake-out tonight?" she asked.

Stanley thought for a moment before replying. "No, I think you were right not to say anything. He would probably have told us not to do it and that it would be a bit of a waste of time. To be honest, Chloe, I think it probably will be. It's highly unlikely that the thieves will be back again and there's nothing left at school to steal unless they want business studies textbooks. If they do want the books, then I'm cancelling the stake-out and leaving it to the police because we would be dealing with some really sick and depraved fugitives."

"At least we are trying to help, Stanley. It's the same with the takeover at school. We're not just lying down, letting these things happen and allowing people to walk all over us," she pointed out. "And tonight will be fun. I haven't sneaked out of the house for ages."

"It won't be fun if my dad finds out. He'll kill me," warned Stanley.

"He's got to catch you first."

They left the police station and headed for home. They still had to make sure they had everything for tonight. On the way they called in at a shop for drinks, chocolate and sweets to keep them going through the night.

Chapter Twenty-Six

"CA-CAW… CA-CAW," CAME the noise through the open bedroom window.

"Chloe," Stanley mouthed in the darkness. Suddenly, his brain came to life as though someone within had triggered a switch. "It's the signal," he reminded himself as his eyes opened and adjusted to his surroundings. He jerked up from his duvet, fully clothed as planned, apart from his shoes. Then he rustled around at the foot of his bed for them and hurriedly tied the laces with fumbling fingers.

"Ca-caw." The noise came once again. Stanley realised for the first time that maybe a sound resembling a parrot wasn't such a good idea for their signal; after all, how many wild parrots were there likely to be in Shigbeth? He peered out of the window and saw Chloe in the shadows of the street. She was hiding behind the gatepost of next door's drive. Stanley waved in her direction and wrestled his rucksack over his shoulder. Gently and carefully, he levered his body out of the window and onto the flat roof of the garage below. From there, it was a short drop down onto the top of the wheelie bin that had been tactically placed there earlier, and then onto the driveway. All in all it took no more than thirty seconds before he was huddled with Chloe behind the gatepost.

"What kept you?" she whispered.

"I was asleep," Stanley replied. "It *is* the middle of the night."

"Come on," she prompted, "we need to get Billy." The two of them scuttled away into the night like a pair of rats.

Billy was already dangling out of his window when they arrived at his house. Thankfully, he didn't need the parrot signal. He launched himself off the ledge and dropped onto the roof slates of the downstairs below. He skidded to a sudden stop before he trod on the guttering.

"What's he doing?" said an alarmed-looking Chloe. "He's going to kill himself if he's not careful."

Billy nudged across the roof like a rubbish cat and steered his way towards the side of the house. He lifted his arms out in front of him and prepared for a risky jump onto a pile of bags, dustbins and wood that lay abandoned adjacent to the garage. The moonlight caught his teeth, revealing a great big silly grin all over his face.

"He's being an idiot," said Chloe.

"Yep," Stanley replied.

"He's going to jump from there?!" said Chloe in alarm.

"Yep," Stanley confirmed.

"He's going to kill himself," speculated Chloe.

"Yes, he is," agreed Stanley.

Billy's smile gleamed. His arms were outstretched.

"He thinks he can fly," said Chloe.

Billy slipped, lost his footing and fell into the bins below with a crash.

"He can't, though," Stanley concluded.

Stanley and Chloe waited for the entire neighbourhood to wake up. Some dogs barked in the distance. After a short pause of silence, Billy emerged from the rubbish, dusting himself down and rubbing his elbow. He shuffled over to join them behind the bush in his front garden.

"Are you okay, Billy?" asked Chloe. "Did you hurt yourself?"

"I'm okay, thanks. I banged my elbow a bit, that's all. I had worse injuries when I was fighting in the war." He nodded.

"What war?" enquired Chloe.

"I was in Vietnam," answered a straight-faced Billy.

Stanley looked at him and wondered if Billy really believed that he had fought in a war that happened some fifty years previously. He then looked at Chloe.

"Are you sure this is a good idea?" he asked.

"Too late now, Stan," she said, and the three of them continued as planned and ran down the street, heading for their stake-out at Shigbeth School.

Chapter Twenty-Seven

LITTLE DID THE three friends know, but as they reached the school another trio of friends were venturing forth on their post-midnight rendezvous on the streets of Shigbeth town. Sidney Rain, Bobby Bathurst and Terry Funk had managed to meet at the job centre as planned earlier that day, in spite of one or two sore heads after their night out at the Rose and Crown where they had made a valiant but futile attempt to try every beer on the menu. Bobby was still alive, having managed to get back and into bed before his much-feared wife returned from another fruitless evening at the bingo hall. Five minutes later and she would have caught him feverishly trying to find the correct key which would grant him access through the front door of the family home.

The three had had a positive time at the job centre. Sidney and Terry had filled out a collection of forms and put their names down for a series of job alerts, meaning that if something came up in their chosen line of work soon, then they would be contacted straight away by email. Bobby helped them complete the details and set the two of them up with email accounts. He even managed to come up with an alibi for his wife regarding their planned night-time activities. A one-night-only driving job would give him an excuse for leaving the house at one o'clock in the morning, and would mean that his wife wouldn't be suspicious and might even be pleased that he was willing to take on work even if it was at uncomfortable, abnormal times of the day. That didn't stop Bobby being worried about dressing up later as a crime-fighting superhero. There was a moment during their lunchtime pub meeting where he came close to backing out of the promise that they had made several hours earlier. Sidney and Terry produced their pieces of the beer mat that they had divided up to symbolise their promise and dedication to the cause, and this had forced Bobby to acknowledge that he too was a man of his word, if only for one night. While his wife was at work and his son at school during the afternoon, he assembled the costume that he had devised and looked at himself in the mirror. Although he was scared stiff that he would turn around to find his wife had returned from work early and was staring at him in horror, there was an excitement beneath the surface too. He was a man of action; his career in the army was testament to that, and of course wearing a uniform had always been quite natural for him. Then again, there is a very thin line between wearing things and looking impressive, and wearing things and looking ridiculous. He still wasn't sure he could go through with this, and that was the first thing that flashed into his mind when his alarm went off in the early hours of the morning.

On the other hand, Terry was very much committed to the cause and eager to live up to the promise that he had made in the pub the night before. His section of beer mat felt like a badge of honour to him, and later he placed it on the mantelpiece in his flat like a family heirloom. Terry had quite enjoyed the events of the last twenty-four hours. A couple of days ago he had been distraught: he had been dismissed from his job and he had lost his favourite stapler. The job in the office at the delivery depot had been his life; other than that, he didn't really have much of one. Contrary to Sidney's crazed beliefs, he never went out at night apart from the odd sojourn to play dominoes at his local pub, and he certainly never frequented the discos and watering holes where the young went to cavort and dance away the early hours. Until yesterday, his only real friend was Houdini, his pet cat, who only really popped home to the flat for food or when it was cold outside. Terry's life had been pretty drab and boring if he was being honest. That had changed suddenly, and he liked it. He had two new friends, and something daring and exciting (if a bit silly) was going to happen that night. He'd enjoyed shopping for the garments he would don as Shigbeth's latest crime-fighting avenger, and for the first time in a long time he admired the reflection in the mirror on his wardrobe door. Later on that evening before he went to bed, he found himself whistling and singing in the shower. He was unemployed, but he was happy. When his alarm clock sprang into action, so did he. It was like Christmas morning as a child, and Terry couldn't get out of bed quick enough.

Sidney's digital watch chimed into life at half past midnight. He'd been in and out of sleep for a few hours. He poked at the silver button on his watch to cancel the alarm. Everything was dark; everything was silent. Sidney rolled the duvet away from his body and heaved himself out of bed. Then, very carefully, he hooked his toes inside his slippers that were strategically positioned at the side of his bed and crept across the bedroom and onto the landing. To his immediate right were the stairs to the downstairs hall. In the opposite direction, back up the landing and past the bathroom, was Stanley's room. Sidney hovered in the silence, checking for sounds. Delicately, he turned away from the stairs and towards Stanley's room. With slow, cautious steps he moved across the landing towards Stanley's door and wrapped his palm around the handle. For a moment he stood there, listening to his own breathing, considering whether to double-check that his son was in there, all wrapped up in his covers and fast asleep as usual. Then his grip on the doorknob loosened. Best not to disturb him, he thought. If he did wake him up then he wouldn't be able to go out tonight, and tonight was the night that he was meeting Bobby and Terry as planned at the water tower. Sidney squeezed his feet inside his slippers and turned round. The carpet on the landing absorbed his steady movements as he nudged towards the stairs. As he descended, the steps failed to register a creaking grumble of complaint due to the extra nails that he had deliberately hammered into the wood years ago to ensure he could move around the house late at night as silent as a phantom. The darkness at the bottom of the stairs swallowed him whole. If Stanley had been there, he would have heard nothing.

In the shower room by the back door, Sidney shed his pyjamas, reached for the kitbag in the cupboard under the sink and quietly climbed into his outfit. Moments later, a figure emerged into the back garden of 71 Bedlam Road, pulling the door closed on exit from the house. A man all in black shrouded by a cloak the colour of the night sky, with dark green boots and a mask hiding his identity from the world. He stole down the tunnel between the garage and the fence, emerging onto the driveway. A fleeting glimpse was available for the world as for a fraction of a second he was lit up by a solitary street light penetrating the darkness. Then in a blink of an eye he was gone, as if he'd only ever existed for a microsecond in the deepest realms of someone's imagination.

Chapter Twenty-Eight

"YOU CAN SEE for miles from up here," shouted Billy from the branch of a tree overlooking Shigbeth School.

"Keep the noise down, Billy," Chloe called back from the base.

Stanley quickly looked around to see if anyone had been disturbed by the two of them calling to each other. There was a row of houses a good stone's throw away through the trees. He breathed a sigh of relief when no lights suddenly flickered on in their windows.

Suddenly, Billy appeared after clambering down from his lofty perch. "You can see for miles from up there," he repeated.

"Yes, we heard you the first time," remarked Stanley. "To be perfectly honest, I think most of the town heard you. We're supposed to be keeping our presence a secret, so if we could stop climbing trees and screaming from the top of them then it would be very much appreciated."

"Sorry," whispered Billy. "I'm a bit excited, that's all. I'll try and be quieter in future."

"It would help if you took that stupid balaclava off from round your head, then you could probably hear better," said Chloe.

"What was that?" asked Billy.

"I said it would probably…" Chloe started, but by the time she had got midway through her repeated instruction, Billy was pulling at his headgear and ripping it away from his ears. He had black streaks of paint all over his cheeks.

"I do hope that paint comes off your face," observed Stanley.

"It's special camouflage paint, Stan. I got it from the government when we did undercover training. With that and my balaclava on, I'm virtually invisible to the enemy."

"Invisible, you say? Standing at the top of a tree, yelling?" Stanley pointed out.

"I've got a great view from up there and I can see everything, especially with my night-vision goggles on. Even at night!"

"I did wonder why they were called night-vision goggles," jeered Stanley. "They just look like a normal pair of binoculars to me, Billy, only someone has stuck red plastic to the lenses."

"State of the art, Stanley; James Bond uses these."

"Billy, you do realise that James Bond is a fictional character, don't you? You do know that he isn't real and is just a figment of someone's imagination?"

"Look, you two, we are supposed to be on a stake-out here," scolded Chloe. "Stop arguing and try and concentrate on keeping an eye out for things."

Stanley had to admit that the position Billy had found them was a pretty good one. They were far enough away from the houses and, covered by trees and bushes, would not be seen or, hopefully, heard. They were also close enough to have a great view of the school car park and canteen, particularly from up the tree where Billy had found a safe perch. A couple of security lights that were attached to walls around the edge of the school building were switched on, which helped them to see certain parts of the school. They would easily be able to see if any classroom lights came on or the headlights of any vehicles suddenly appeared in view.

Chloe reached inside her bag for a jumper. It wasn't the warmest of nights and a mist had started to descend, leaving beads of moisture on the grass and on their clothes. As she retrieved her extra layer, she also pulled out a small rug which she laid on the dampening floor to sit on.

"Have you got anything to eat?" asked Stanley.

Chloe pulled out a stash of chocolate bars and stood there waiting for gasps of admiration as if she was a magician pulling a rabbit out of a hat. Billy declined the offer and went scuttling back up the tree to keep up the surveillance. Chloe folded herself cross-legged on the rug and Stanley joined her as they both munched on their confectionery.

"I'm not staying here all night, Chloe," said Stanley. "If my dad catches me then I'll be in big trouble."

"Don't worry, Stanley; if it stays this cold and the drizzle keeps on getting worse then I won't be out much longer either," she replied. "You're not the only one who will end up getting killed or grounded if we get caught."

Stanley and Chloe sat shoulder to shoulder on the rug, feeling the rain in the air settle on their faces.

"Nothing's going to happen tonight, Chloe. Whoever robbed the school won't be coming back again, not unless they are completely stupid."

"I know that, Stan," admitted Chloe.

"Then why are we here risking getting into massive amounts of trouble with our parents, sitting in the rain and the dark under a tree?"

"I do realise that it's highly unlikely that we'll catch the thieves and get the computers back, but I just feel as though we need to do something, even if it is wasting our time being stuck out in the early hours like this. Staying at home in bed just seems like we're letting it happen. Do you understand?"

"I think so. You also realise that the school is being taken over whether you like it or not, and that we'll all be wearing those stupid uniforms and basketball club will still be getting cancelled because other events will be going on in the gym?

We can organise petitions and film things and complain until we are blue in the face, but it won't change anything. Greenstock Academy has already happened, Chloe."

"I know that too, Stanley, but we can't just let it pass without our feelings being made known. These important people in powerful jobs and positions make decisions which affect our lives and go through with them without considering how we might feel. Then they claim that they are doing it for us, but in reality they are doing it simply because it suits them. How can we not be asked about changes to our school when school is the most important thing in our lives? We're moved around like pieces on a chessboard, Stanley, and it's not right."

Stanley nodded. "As long as you realise that nothing will change and our efforts are in vain, then that's okay. I don't want you to get upset or hurt, Chloe, that's all."

Chloe smiled back at him. Beads of rain were parachuting at intervals from her fringe onto her nose. "Anyway, Stanley Rain, why are you out here in the dark if you are so aware that you are wasting your time?" she asked.

"I'm not wasting my time, Chloe. I'm with you," he responded.

They held each other's gaze for a moment and she linked his arm with hers before resting her head against his chest. Then something fell out of the sky.

Unfortunately (or so thought Stanley) it wasn't Billy; although he wasn't far behind, clambering down the tree to recover what he had dropped from on high.

"Sorry, team, but I dropped my torch."

"You were lucky it didn't land on our heads," admonished Chloe.

Billy was more bothered about finding the lost piece of kit than worrying about his comrades. He ferreted around in the grass and bushes at the base of the tree. "Don't worry, guys, I've found it," he cheered.

"Oh, I'm so pleased," Stanley chided.

"Glad I've found it, though. It's an agency torch, government issue, solar powered," Billy proclaimed.

"How can you have a solar-powered torch," asked Stanley, "when there's not any sunshine around at this time of night to power it?"

"I don't know, but they get hold of all the latest technology and pass it on to their agents in the field. A bit like my titanium sunglasses and my walkie-talkie that has an unlimited range; you can travel to the other side of the world with that and still hear the other person on the other unit talking to you, crystal clear like they're stood right next to you." Billy flicked the torch on and shone it up at his face so he was lit up like a lantern. His eyes and teeth shone in the light, in between the camouflage paint streaked across his cheeks and into his spiky hair.

"Look, Billy, we'd love to stay here all night long but we can't," confessed Stanley.

"We've got to go home at some point, Billy," reasoned Chloe. "It's getting cold and we've got school in the morning. We also need to get back in bed before our parents get up."

"That's okay," said Billy. "I do appreciate that you guys haven't benefited from all the training I've done in counter-espionage over the years. I sometimes forget that this isn't the sort of work that comes naturally to people. I'm planning on staying here all night until breakfast time. I might pop home later on to get my school uniform on and have a little wee, but not just yet. I'll keep watch till then. You guys go on back to base and get some rest. Leave it to the experts."

"Thanks, Billy," said Chloe, rubbing her hands up and down her shoulders to ward off the invading cold air.

"What if something happens?" Billy suddenly thought. "What if the thieves come back?"

"Well, what about the walkie-talkie, Billy? If you let one of us take one, then you could call in an emergency, couldn't you? Surely it will still have a signal over by my house?" said Chloe. Billy immediately started searching his backpack for the required item.

"Didn't you hear Billy earlier?" mocked Stanley. "It has an unlimited range. You could go to another galaxy and you'd still be able to talk to him."

"Here it is," said Billy, handing it over. "Just press the talk button wherever you are, and we can communicate if there's an emergency."

Chloe studied the walkie-talkie unit as Billy placed it in her outstretched palm. "Are you sure this is government issue?" she asked. "Only, it has a Spider-Man badge and picture on it. It looks like a toy."

Stanley examined it and laughed.

"Of course it does, Chloe. That's deliberate in case the enemy find it; that's exactly what they would think too." Billy tapped the end of his nose with his finger, as if he was 'in the know' about something that was top secret.

Chloe and Stanley said their goodbyes and left Billy to his own devices in the tree overlooking Shigbeth School. They tried the walkie-talkie as they left the line of trees circumventing the school playing field and headed away back down the main road. There was no answer from Billy; just a prolonged buzz of interference. The range of the government-issue technology had barely lasted a couple of hundred metres. At a suitable point, the two friends separated and made their own ways back towards their welcoming beds. All in Shigbeth was quiet for now as the town sat in the dark and the damp, waiting for the dawn of a new day and the hustle and bustle that it would undoubtedly bring.

Chapter Twenty-Nine

ON THE OTHER side of town, the Raven stood in the shadows at the foot of the giant water tower, awaiting his guests. This was the place where Sidney was due to meet the others if they came good on their promises and dared to join him in his nocturnal adventure. He was reasonably confident that Terry would show; he had seemed so keen when they discussed their rendezvous earlier in the day. However, he feared that Bobby would give in to logic and common sense and wouldn't go through with the solemn promise he had made when he accepted the piece of beer mat the other night at the Rose and Crown. Besides, there was a chill in the air tonight and a drizzly rain threatened to make a trip out beyond midnight uncomfortable for those used to curling up, cosy and warm, in their beds rather than daring to brave the outside world.

Suddenly, there was a shuffling of feet across the small, empty car park beyond the base of the water tower, and Sidney noticed a flicker of contrast through a gap in the broken wall out to his left. Someone else was out at night. Someone was coming.

"Sidney? Sidney?" came a hushed call.

"I'm the Raven, not Sidney."

"Oh yeah, sorry, Sidney – I mean Raven," replied Terry Funk.

Sidney was trying to fathom out what on earth his friend was wearing when a hand tapped him on his right shoulder and made him jump. He spun round instantly, hands raised at the ready to deal with an assailant, only to see what he thought was Bobby Bathurst dressed in brown from head to toe.

"Crept up on you without you knowing didn't I?" asked Bobby.

Sidney got his breath back. "I knew you were there all along."

"Is that why you jumped six foot in the air when I put my hand on your shoulder?" teased Bobby.

"You two look great," said Terry from beneath what appeared to be a cycling helmet and a pair of swimming goggles.

"Thanks, Terry, but I feel like I've arrived at a fancy-dress party kitted out in a prat costume," replied Bobby.

"What in God's name are you wearing, Terry?" enquired Sidney.

"Well, you told us that we needed to go away and create a crime-fighting identity like in the comic books, and here I am."

Sidney reached for his head torch and switched it on so that he could get a better idea of what Terry was wearing. He was dressed in black. He had a black cycling helmet on his head, a black tracksuit top with white stripes down the sides of his arms, black cargo trousers and a pair of black trainers on his feet, again with white stripes on. In the middle of his face he wore a pair of swimming goggles rather than his usual thick-rimmed spectacles. They made his eyes seem huge, just like those of a fish.

"Blinking Nora," observed Bobby with his mouth wide open.

"Who are you supposed to be?" asked Sidney, pulling back his bird mask to reveal a worried look of concern.

Terry did a twirl, like a matador entering the centre of a bullring, and flapped the black cloak that was wrapped around his neck behind him as he pirouetted. In the middle of the cloak, running down it lengthways was a thick white stripe.

"Black with white stripes and out at night. Isn't it obvious?"

Sidney and Bobby examined him up and down and then looked at each other.

"No idea," concluded Sidney.

"It's an animal, and it rhymes with my surname too?" prompted Terry, hoping that these clues would give the game away.

Sidney and Bobby still hadn't a clue what he was supposed to be.

“I’m Skunk,” Terry stated proudly.

“You’re mental,” suggested Bobby.

“Come to mention it, now I’ve seen the swimming goggles it’s pretty clear to me,” added Sidney sarcastically.

“Do skunks ride bikes these days?” asked Bobby, pointing at the cycling helmet on top of Terry’s head.

“The bicycle helmet is black like a skunk and hides my head, as well as being a safety measure, and the goggles help me to have the beady eyes of a skunk and again are useful in hiding my identity, and in case we have to pursue someone underwater,” responded Terry. “And I’ve loads of equipment in the pockets of my cargo trousers,” he added, delving his gloved hands into them.

“Are those oven gloves?” asked Bobby.

“They were, but I cunningly cut them in two and they also fit in with my new Skunk persona, as not only are they jet black again, but they are padded in case I have to punch anyone, and they’ll be good for things like digging if we need to make a getaway. But you know what a skunk’s main weapon is, don’t you?”

“They stink,” offered Bobby, turning up his nose at the same time.

“Exactly, Bobby, correctamundo.” Terry took his hand out of one of his multitude of trouser pockets and held out his hand. In his palm were a number of small plastic balls.

“What the devil are they?” asked Sidney.

"They're stink bombs, Sidney. I went down the joke shop in town and got these babies. I accidentally dropped one in the house earlier and it stunk the place out. I had to evacuate into the back garden and the neighbour next door called for the plumber to get her drains checked out." Terry smiled and put them away carefully in a zipped trouser pocket.

"Okay, Terry... I mean Skunk. We've seen you, now let's see about you, Bobby," said Sidney.

Sidney and Terry's eyes locked on their new target. A very brown Bobby Bathurst stood in front of them with the light from Sidney's head torch glaring into his eyes. Bobby's cheeks were smeared with some sort of brown, black and green camouflage paint.

"Who are you supposed to be, Bobby?" asked Terry.

"I feel stupid," Bobby admitted.

"You don't look stupid at all," encouraged Terry, "does he, Sidney?"

Sidney was about to disagree until Terry nudged him with his elbow. "No, you don't look stupid at all, Bobby, lad."

Bobby looked like a grown man, desperately trying to come to terms with the fact that he was hanging about an industrial estate at one o'clock in the morning in a costume with paint smeared all over his face. He had a brown cap on which he wore back to front, and was dressed in brown overalls, the type usually worn by people like removal men. He had brown leather walking boots on his feet, and a cloak on his back which appeared to be a tweedy type of sackcloth. Attached at the back of this were what looked like two broom heads.

"I'm Squirrel," he announced. "Sergeant Squirrel."

Sidney bit his lip, trying very hard not to laugh. A huge grin crept across his face.

"Sergeant Squirrel?" said Terry.

"Yes," confirmed Bobby. "Got any questions?"

Sidney coughed into his glove, trying to hide his amusement at Bobby's newly devised character.

"I've got a couple, Bobby, if you don't mind?" asked Terry. "Firstly, why did you go for the squirrel look?"

Bobby's eyes peered out from behind the face paint and beneath the brown cap that rested back to front on top of his grey hair. "Well, I suppose I had lots of brown stuff to wear, so I immediately thought of a squirrel."

Both Terry and Sidney seemed unconvinced by the explanation.

"Squirrels aren't brown, they are typically grey in this country," Terry pointed out.

"Well, the ones I've seen have always been brown. And anyway, squirrels are elusive, fast and good at climbing, a bit like me really," he added. "I've even got a bushy tail that I put together by sawing off the ends of a couple of brooms that I found in the shed. Although, they do bang together a bit when I run and make a knocking sound, so I might have to rethink that one."

Terry studied the hem of Sergeant Squirrel's sackcloth cape to see the bristles that Bobby was talking about reviewing. Bobby lifted the cape as if curtseying for the Queen so that the offending items could be seen more easily.

"And my second question is why *Sergeant* Squirrel?" Terry continued. "After all, I'm just Skunk and he's just the Raven."

Sidney nodded in support of the line of questioning.

"Well, I used to be a sergeant in the army and so it just seemed to feel right. Besides, lots of superheroes have formal titles and army ranks preceding their names."

"Such as who?" asked Sidney.

"Well, there's Captain America," replied Bobby.

"Who else?" asked Terry.

Bobby was deep in thought. They all were. No such example entered any of their minds.

"I don't know exactly, but there are loads. So Sergeant Squirrel it is," affirmed Bobby.

The three friends stood there underneath the water tower in silence looking at each other's outfits with a degree of disbelief.

"Right then, Sergeant Squirrel and Skunk. Let's show you round town," the Raven invited. "We'll start with a view of Shigbeth." He pulled down his bird mask and started to fix the head torch around the top. "Follow me," he cried, and made for the metal ladder at the base of the landmark that towered above them. "Let's see how good squirrels and skunks are at climbing."

Chapter Thirty

FOR THE NEXT hour, the Raven led his new comrades on a tour of the town. They took in the vista of Shigbeth from the summit of the water tower, although tonight their view was slightly hampered by the growing cloud and the waves of light rain that pitched in on the breeze. They dodged down side streets and around the empty allotments on Berrington Drive, which during the day were a hive of activity with pensioners pulling potatoes out of the soil whilst complaining about the latest aches and pains in their stiffening bodies. They ducked in and out of the shadows of street lights via the backs of the usually bustling shops on Waterhouse Row. The odd taxi screeched past, unknowing that hidden in the dark by walls and fences, or crouched in the shroud of night behind wheelie bins and trees, were three grown adults in costume. They stood in the middle of Warchester Park with the clock tower at its heart emerging from the rain like a spectral lighthouse, to catch their breath at the steps circling the foot of the monument and soak in the eerie silence of the gardens that were devoid of the chatter, dogs and balls that brought them to life during daylight.

"What do you think?" asked the Raven, his ribcage moving in and out like an accordion.

"It's fantastic," replied Skunk, removing his swimming goggles for a second. "I've not had as much fun as this for ages."

"And you, Sergeant Squirrel?"

"Well, if I'm being honest, it was fifty-fifty whether or not I was going to come tonight. I wasn't sure about lying to the wife about what I was doing and where I was going. I also looked at myself in the mirror before I left and just felt like a complete muppet. And I don't mind admitting I was shaking a little as I headed out because I was worried about being seen and laughed at, or even worse, arrested by the police and put in a lunatic asylum."

"And how do you feel now?" asked Skunk.

"I hate to admit it but I'm actually rather enjoying myself. I don't know what it is, but I feel sort of… I don't know… sort of…"

"Free?" The Raven finished his sentence for him.

"Yes, that's exactly it. Free; like I've been let off a lead or something. I feel a little like I did when I was in the army; all this running around and ducking down behind things, it's like the old times again. I feel younger. I feel like I did when I was a child. Before I had to grow up and be responsible."

"Told you that you wouldn't regret it," said the Raven. "And also, you don't have to worry about being seen. I know all the places to go and not to go and how to keep hidden. There's rarely anybody out at this time of night. The world's fast asleep."

Skunk was fastening his swimming goggles back onto his face, which was now wet with the falling rain. "We haven't solved any crimes, though, or seen any action, have we?" he noted.

"No, but that doesn't happen often because there isn't much of it about. Besides, that's not the point," responded the Raven.

"What do you mean, Sidney?"

"Well, it's nice to think that just by being here, we're keeping things safe." Sidney's Raven mask was perched on his chest and he took a moment to wipe the rain from his face with his sleeve. "It's like everyone who's asleep is able to sleep soundly, safe in the knowledge that there are people out here protecting them."

"You mean, like, sort of guardian angels?"

"Yes, Terry, I suppose a little bit like that."

"But people don't know that we're out here looking after them," said Bobby.

"No, but that's okay by me and I very much hope that we remain anonymous and don't get found out. If we do get caught then that will have to be the end of this," answered Sidney. "Anyway, boys, are we ready to move? Time's short and we ought to think about turning in for the night soon."

"We need a signal or something for when we move into action," suggested Bobby.

"Such as what?"

"I've got an idea," revealed Terry. "Let's form a circle and all place a hand on top of each other's."

Sidney and Bobby both looked puzzled.

"Come on, do as you're told," instructed Terry.

The three men stood under the watchful gaze of Warchester Park's clock tower and each laid a hand over the previous one.

"My hand needs to go on the bottom," suggested the Raven, "because I founded the group."

"What are we going to call ourselves?" asked Sergeant Squirrel.

The Raven's eyes lit up behind his bird mask. "I've got it. We're going to call ourselves the Shigbeth Justice League, like the guys in the comics."

Sergeant Squirrel wasn't entirely convinced. "Are you sure? It sounds a bit naff."

"I like it," said Skunk. "The Shigbeth Justice League."

"Anyway, I founded the group and so I get to decide what it's called. Shigbeth Justice League it is," stated the Raven.

All three nodded in acceptance. Skunk grinned from ear to ear.

"This is what we'll do, then. With our hands lying on top of each other, one of us shouts, 'Shigbeth', then the next shouts, 'Justice', and the third shouts, 'League'. Then we all head off."

"That sounds weird," concluded Sergeant Squirrel.

"Let's try it at least," said Skunk.

The newly named Shigbeth Justice League all reached their hands into the middle of the circle, with the Raven making sure that his hand was first and on the bottom of the pile.

"Shigbeth," called the Raven.

"Justice," shouted Skunk.

"League," finished Sergeant Squirrel.

"Disengage!" added Skunk.

"What was that?" asked Sergeant Squirrel.

"I added something dynamic at the end, like a command word. Makes it more exciting, doesn't it?"

"I should be doing that," argued the Raven. "After all, I founded the group."

"Yes, but it was me that came up with the idea of the team chant, and of adding an extra command word at the end," replied Skunk.

"I'll do it if you two are going to argue about it," offered Sergeant Squirrel. "Your hand's on the bottom anyway, Sidney, so you've already got your own way on something."

"My hand's on the bottom because I was the one who founded the group."

"Are you going to bang on about that all night? That's the hundredth time I've heard about you founding the group already."

"Well I did, and anyway I've only mentioned it about four times."

"Yeah, four times in the last minute."

"It was hundreds of times, you said just now."

Skunk interrupted the growing confrontation. "Look, guys, we shouldn't be arguing about this. We are a team after all, and that's really what the team chant is all about: three forces uniting as one. We could always take it in turns."

"I should go first because I founded the group," said the Raven.

Sergeant Squirrel tutted and looked up to the sky.

"Hands together, boys," the Raven instructed. The other two placed their hands together on top of his. Sergeant Squirrel's hand was placed, somewhat reluctantly, on top of Skunk's.

"Shigbeth," called the Raven.

"Justice," shouted Skunk.

"League," finished Sergeant Squirrel.

"Go!" added Sidney.

The group separated on the Raven's instruction.

"Go? Is that the best that you can come up with?" asked Sergeant Squirrel.

"I'd like to see you come up with better," replied the Raven.

The three joined their hands again in the middle for another go.

"Shigbeth," called the Raven.

"Justice," shouted Skunk.

"League," finished Sergeant Squirrel. "Move off!"

It was Skunk this time that was provoked into a response. "Move off? Go? You two are useless at this. You should be shouting impressive things as command words. Nobody's going to be impressed with things like that. You need to use your imagination and come up with things that make us sound exciting and technical and like we have plans about what we are going to do."

"Such as what?" asked the Raven.

"Like 'Operation Action Force', or 'City of Freedom', or 'Task Force Rising', or 'Code Name Octopus', or 'Strike Back Danger', or 'Call to Arms', or something that paints an image that suggests we are more than three silly men dressed up in daft costumes; that suggests we are professionals, not amateurs."

Sidney and Bobby stood there in realisation that Terry was actually quite good at this.

"You're in charge of command words, Terry," said Sergeant Squirrel. The Raven nodded in agreement and the Shigbeth Justice League pressed their palms on top of each other again.

"Shigbeth," called the Raven.

"Justice," shouted Skunk.

"League," finished Sergeant Squirrel.

"Park Patrol Enforcement!" added Skunk.

The group sped off together, away from the centre of the park. They all had big grins on their faces, and their capes fluttered behind them as they ran. In the darkness all you could hear was the rasping of their breath as they jogged and the tapping of the broom heads at the bottom of Sergeant Squirrel's cloak, bashing together as his legs moved.

Chapter Thirty-One

BY THE TIME the dynamic trio had reached the outskirts of the park, their jogging had slowed to a halt. All were only too aware of how unfit they were, and some of the talk had turned to how they might improve their physical capabilities in the coming weeks. As they strolled through the children's adventure playground, they suddenly heard a clattering from the vicinity of the wooden pirate ship. All three stopped and looked for somewhere to hide, but the truth of the matter was that they were out in the open and so if there was someone there, then they would have a potential view of the three of them, albeit compromised by the lack of light.

A voice then called at them from across the playground. "Raven, man, is that you?"

"Calvin?" Sidney relaxed, and the others clung to the idea that their discovery wasn't necessarily as bad as they might have feared.

"Yeah, it's me, innit!" came the response. A scruffy, bedraggled figure started to emerge from inside the pirate ship, making his way over to where the three observers were stood. He rubbed his eyes and scratched his beard, the bobble on the top of his hat positioned like a bauble on a Christmas tree.

"How are you, my good friend?" the Raven greeted him.

"I'm all right, thanks, my main man. Just been getting some shut-eye in the old *Black Flag*, keeping out of the rain a bit," responded Calvin. "What's with the new guys, Raven, man? Who are the friends you bringing?"

"Gentlemen, this is my good friend Calvin. Please introduce yourselves."

It was an awkward moment as for the first time the other two members of the Shigbeth Justice League confirmed their identities to a stranger.

Terry stepped forward first, with rain dripping off his black cycle helmet and his swimming goggles partly fogged up with condensation. "I'm Skunk." The white stripes on his arms and footwear stood out against the pitch black.

Bobby stepped into view, and placed his hands on his hips. He put on a surprisingly deep voice. "And I'm Sergeant Squirrel," he confessed boldly.

Calvin burst into laughter and reached in his pocket for a hip flask. He took a swig and his eyes bulged in their sockets. "Whoa, there's loads of you guys. I'm going back down the off-licence tomorrow and getting me some more of this rocket fuel before word gets around and they sell out. This is some crazy stuff going on."

"Calvin is one of my top informants," the Raven announced proudly.

"You mean there are others?" asked Skunk.

"Actually, if I'm being honest, no, there's not. He's my only top informant."

The Raven turned to face Calvin who was staring at the three of them in awe. "So what have you got for me from the old grapevine, Calvin?"

"Eh?" replied a bemused Calvin.

The Raven pressed on. "What have you heard on the jungle drums, my friend?"

Calvin stared back, obviously a little bit confused at the line of questioning. The Raven shuffled his feet and tried again, aware of the audience he was trying desperately to impress.

"Have you got any nuggets for me?" he insisted.

Calvin gestured to his empty pockets. "Raven, man, I haven't got anything to eat, and it's ages since I've been to McDonald's anyway."

"No, I mean have you got any information for me?" Sidney was a bit embarrassed at the misunderstanding, and also because he didn't have any money with him tonight to pay Calvin for the supposed information that he would usually give him in return. *One of the many disadvantages of being unemployed*, he thought for a moment.

The penny finally seemed to drop with Calvin,

however. "No, Raven, man, I ain't got any juicy bits to tell you of tonight. It's been raining too much for me to be out and about. I haven't seen anything since I told you about that truck down by the school the other night."

Sidney was puzzled. He didn't remember anything about a truck at the school.

"What do you mean, Calvin? What truck?"

"I told you about the suspicious truck hanging around at the school the other night. Don't you remember, Raven?"

The truth was that Sidney couldn't really remember much at all about that night, apart from the fact that he was indeed down near the school. That's where he fell off the wall and banged his head and the old man had come to his aid.

"You okay, Sid… I mean Raven?" enquired Skunk.

Sidney was lost in thought. "Yes, I'm fine… oh yes, I remember now," he lied in a bid to save face.

"Too late for them, eh?" asked Calvin, scratching his grey beard.

"Yes, whatever they were up to, they'd scarpered by the time I got there. Probably saw me coming and fled."

There was a pause as Sidney recovered his train of thought and the other members of the Justice League waited for his lead. Calvin continued to stare at the collection of costumes in front of him, a look of amazement etched on his wrinkled face.

"Well, come on then, team, we need to make a move," said Sidney, moving his hand into the middle of his colleagues, ready for the team chant.

"Shigbeth," he began.

"Justice," responded Skunk.

"League," added Sergeant Squirrel.

"Adventure Zone Crescendo!" shouted Skunk, and the three set off again, away from the park, waving at Calvin as they departed, apart from Sergeant Squirrel who gave an army-style salute from his back-to-front cap.

Calvin waved back, and then started a wobbly retreat to the hull of his chosen shelter for the night. "I do not believe it," he yelled as he walked. "That is one crazy dream I have just been having. And people keep telling me that I should give up drinking, innit!"

Chapter Thirty-Two

"YOU LOOK AS though you've been up all night," remarked Chloe as she met Stanley at the usual street corner before heading into school.

Right on cue, Stanley yawned in response.

"You didn't get caught sneaking back in, then?" she asked.

"No way, it was easier than I thought. My dad is still sleeping in this morning, yet again. He shouted down for a cup of tea from his bedroom and told me to help myself to muesli in the kitchen," replied Stanley.

"He's still on his health kick, then?"

"Yes a bit of one I think, but it's not really working. He's been spending more time than ever in bed and he's been suffering with his stomach and his back already this week. I reckon his system is rejecting some of the stuff like muesli that he simply isn't used to. I'm a bit worried about him."

"My mum really likes him, though. She hasn't stopped talking about him since he came round looking for you and moved that pot plant for her. She says he's got lovely muscles and that I should invite you round for tea and a sleepover so that she gets the chance to meet him again."

Stanley was quite pleased about the idea of staying over at Chloe's house, but was unsure how Miss Scott had got the idea that his dad was gorgeous and rippling with muscles.

"Sounds like your dad finally got round to joining the gym."

"Join a gym?!" Stanley reacted with incredulity. "My dad can't even lift himself out of bed at the moment, let alone lift any weights. When he does eventually get up it would be great if he went shopping and got some proper food in the house, and got the van back so I can get a lift to school now and again."

"Do you not want to walk to school with me, Stanley?" said Chloe.

"No, it's not that, Chloe, it's just sometimes we could get a lift, say, if it's raining or something," he explained hurriedly.

As the two friends arrived at the school gates, something nearly as troubling as the police cars from earlier in the week greeted them. A huge plastic banner had been put up by the car park advertising that Shigbeth School would soon become Greenstock Academy. The new school motto of *Aspire, acquire, attire* was emblazoned across it, with a picture of two smiling students in the new uniform. Betwixt the two students was a photograph of a smirking Nigel Greenstock with his hair slicked back as if an oil tanker had emptied its contents all over his head.

"I don't believe it," said a disgusted Chloe.

"Blimey. I suppose we ought to get that petition launched this morning, Chloe. Things are moving fast." warned Stanley.

"I'll start collecting names at morning break," she said.

As they stood staring at the grinning face of Nigel Greenstock, Billy sprang into view, running towards them from inside the school.

"Stanley, Chloe – great news!" He slid to a halt directly in front of them, having bounded up to them like an excited puppy.

"Did you see something after we left you last night, Billy?" asked Chloe hopefully.

"Last night? No, nothing happened so I went home earlier than planned, but I was in school really early this morning because I couldn't get back to sleep. I saw them putting the banner up and everything. We're getting some more computers. I've just seen them – well, I haven't actually seen them because they are still in their boxes, but Mrs Jeeraz says that they are new and for us to use later this week."

"Great – that means I can start doing that community film about the takeover of the school. Maybe we could film some interviews to show what the children really feel about what is going on?" Chloe thought out loud.

"Yes, and you know what it also means?" asked Billy. "I get Billy 2000 Junior and his dad back too," he replied, answering his own question.

"They won't actually be the Billy 2000s, though, will they, Billy, if they're brand new?" Stanley pointed out.

"No, they won't, but maybe they could be related. I could call the iPad Brother of Billy 2000 Junior or something like that."

"Are we getting the new computers to replace the old ones that were stolen, then?" enquired Stanley.

"No, Mrs Jeeraz told me that there was an order that got sort of stuck in the post, and those are the ones that finally arrived first thing this morning," Billy informed them, finally getting his breath back after all the excitement at his breaking news.

"Well, that's some good news at last, I suppose. No more business studies out of those boring old textbooks," Stanley remarked.

Unfortunately, they did spend some of the morning completing work out of the boring old business studies textbooks as the new computers remained cocooned in their boxes. At break time, Chloe started collecting names for the petition that she eventually planned to send off to the school governors, the local MP and the *Shigbeth Gazette*. There were quite a few names on it by the time they were called back in to lessons. Some students agreed with her that they should have been consulted about the impending changes, whereas others signed it simply because they were asked to do so, which Stanley felt was a little worrying.

Over lunch, Chloe and Stanley continued their determined quest to add even more names to the petition, but their plans were hampered by a change in the weather. Showers started to roll in and that meant the students weren't spread out across the playground and field, where they could easily be approached about their thoughts regarding the conversion of the school into the academy. The consequence of the gloomy weather outside was that students preferred to stay indoors and the school became a crowded mass of girls and boys littering classrooms and corridors. Furthermore, with teachers around indoors too it was more difficult to add names to the list surreptitiously without arousing suspicion as to what they were doing. There was the worry that if some of the teachers found out they would inevitably have to report it to Miss Tyler, and that would result in serious trouble. Having said that, both Chloe and Stanley felt that many of the teachers would, at least in principle, support the action they were taking. Chloe did think about recruiting someone like Mrs Jeeraz to the cause, but Stanley felt it wasn't worth the risk and that they should just resolve to concentrate on presenting the students' perspective on the issue.

Chapter Thirty-Three

THE RAIN WAS still falling when the PE lesson started up in the afternoon. Stanley didn't look forward to PE because all the boys had to queue outside in a line to be registered. Normally a little wait would be just about bearable, but today of course the weather wasn't pleasant and so Stanley and Billy stood there in the rain getting steadily wetter and wetter.

"It's not fair. It's sexist," suggested Billy, with raindrops leaping off the bridge of his nose and his spiky hair wilting under the weight of the water. "It's all right for the girls, they get to go in straight away and get changed. And they're probably doing PE in the hall today. They'll be doing dance or something in the warmth while we have to do rugby outside."

Stanley didn't respond. He was too wet to offer a supportive or alternative comment, and he was tired after spending half the night on surveillance duty in case the computer thieves miraculously came back. *As if they would*, he thought to himself. Instead, he waited for the emergence of the PE teacher Mr Webster at the entrance to the changing rooms. As usual, he was probably still inside the PE office, watching television, slurping tea and munching on chocolate digestives. Mr Webster was not a good example to the students on how to look after your physique and keep yourself fit and healthy. Firstly, he was asthmatic and was always having to use his inhaler. Secondly, he was very round, with his stomach hanging over the top of his tracksuit bottoms like it was trying to escape from his body. Overall, he was the laziest teacher in the school and his sole mission in life was to do as little as possible and to make life for himself as comfortable as he could. As a result, PE lessons were hard and dull; nothing fun ever happened. They reminded Stanley of geography, but at least that was indoors in a classroom.

Finally, Mr Webster emerged, almost as if he was waiting around the corner until it reached the point when the waiting students couldn't possibly get any wetter. Typically, he was wrapped up in a tracksuit and a waterproof jacket and had a huge golf umbrella projected above him like a parachute. Stanley and Billy were cold, wet and about to get changed into their shorts and head out onto the field.

"What's going on here?" asked Webster in his gravelly voice that always seemed as though he was gasping for air. Immediately, he reached for his asthma inhaler and readied it for use. "This needs sorting out," he announced. Mr Webster used the words 'sorting and sorted' a lot. They were his favourite words, but no one ever knew how to respond when he asked for things to be 'sorted out'.

"Right, let's get sorted then," he commanded.

Nobody moved, mostly because the students still didn't understand what exactly 'let's get sorted' actually meant. Webster sucked on his inhaler and started to read out the register. A few more minutes of standing outside in the rain followed before the register was completed.

"Right then, boys, we can't use the sports hall today because it's being used for a wedding fair and fashion show over the next few nights. That means, after you've got changed into your PE kit, we're on the field doing rugby."

Richie 'Thicky' Drinkwater raised his hand in the air.

"What is it, Drinkwater?" asked Mr Webster.

"It's raining, Mr Webster," Richie stated.

"What are you, a weather forecaster, Drinkwater? I do realise it's raining. Maybe you noticed the whacking great umbrella above my head? Bit of a clue, isn't it, son? You can play rugby in the rain, you know. A bit of water never hurt anyone. Now, let's get this sorted. I want you out in the middle of the field within five minutes. And if any of you are wearing jumpers underneath your tops to keep warm, then you'll be in detention after school." Mr Webster sucked on his inhaler again. "Right, boys, sort it."

Everyone made a beeline for the changing rooms; at least they would be dry in there for a few minutes. When they emerged into the rain after getting changed, Stanley and Billy were surprised to see the girls out on the field in the rain too, knocking balls to each other with hockey sticks. Chloe looked furious as they passed, her hair matted over her face, wringing wet already from head to toe.

"How come you aren't inside?" asked Billy.

Chloe's face screwed up in anger and eyes burned fiercely. "Because the sports hall is being used for a wedding-fair-cum-fashion-show and the school hall is being prepared for drinks and nibbles for a business meeting after school."

Stanley didn't dare say anything in response as he wasn't entirely sure whether they were drops of rains running down her face or tears of anger and frustration. Chloe gave a hockey ball a huge thwack, sending it a good few metres past the girl she was supposed to be passing to.

In the middle of the field, Mr Webster stood there under his great blue-and-white umbrella, all wrapped up in his warm tracksuit and jacket. He'd even brought a flask of tea with him to drink as he watched the boys throw rugby balls to each other, which wasn't easy due to the slippery conditions. Every so often he would issue orders from underneath his brolly. Eventually, the rain eased off and the class moved on to practising tackling; again not ideal because of the damp grass and a general reluctance from everyone to get muddy.

Mr Webster tentatively decided to come out from his shelter, checking for rain first just in case he got wet, and illustrate how it was done. Richie 'Thicky' Drinkwater was naturally chosen as the victim; he always seemed to be in the wrong place at the wrong time.

"Right, boys, I've been watching you and your tackling's rubbish. Some of you would struggle to play for Wales, the way you are performing; it's that bad. I'm going to show you how it's done," he proclaimed in his wheezy, reedy voice. "Drinkwater, I want you to run towards me with the ball."

"Are you sure, Sir?" replied a frightened Richie.

"Come on, it's perfectly safe. Just run at me with the ball, Drinkwater; stop mucking about."

Thicky set off tentatively at first towards Mr Webster, and then broke into a jog. As he got closer, Mr Webster suddenly reared up and gave out a huge, dinosaur-like roar. Richie dropped the ball and cowered.

"Lesson number one is be aggressive when you are tackling. Get into the other player's mind," he shouted, pointing his forefinger at the side of his head. "Right, Drinkwater, you were useless there so get down in the mud and give me twenty press-ups. Let's try it again with someone else."

Billy Bathurst was the only student in the class to put his hand up. Everybody looked at him as if he was mad.

"Right, Bathurst, your turn, sunshine," invited Webster. "You need to get past me, and please do a better job than Drinkwater did."

Billy cradled a rugby ball to his chest. He walked over to his starting point and then started to move towards Mr Webster with a little more speed and determination than the previous victim. As he inched closer, he stepped to the right and, with a little burst of speed, he looked as though he was going to avoid the teacher. There was a hint of a smile on Billy's face as for a moment he thought he was in the clear. Unfortunately for him, Mr Webster used his outstretched boot to trip Billy's trailing leg, and Billy landed face first in the mud.

"Lesson number two; do whatever it takes to stop your opponent. Now, in the game of rugby what just happened was illegal, but that isn't the point. You must have the mentality to stop your opponent with whatever weapons you have at your disposal. If I'd had a shotgun just then, then make no mistake, I would have used it on Bathurst."

The boys stood there worrying about who would be next. Richie collapsed in the mud as he got close to double figures in his press-ups. Billy was sat on the grass looking like he had earlier that morning, only with mud smeared all over his face rather than camouflage paint. Fortunately, the girls then started walking past, making their way back to the changing rooms, prompting Mr Webster to call for the end of the session. Chloe strode over to Stanley.

"I've just about had enough of this, Stan. I'm going to see Miss Tyler right after I've got showered and changed. We have had to do PE in the pouring rain while the halls are being used for stupid business things that are nothing to do with the school. I'm going to tell Tyler that this school should be run in the interests of the children, not for the likes of Nigel Greenstock."

"Are you sure that's wise, Chloe?" asked Stanley.

"What do you mean?" she replied.

"Well, we haven't got the petition finished yet and I can see that you are angry, so perhaps now isn't the best moment to go storming into Miss Tyler's office, that's all," explained Stanley.

"When *is* the best time, Stanley; next week, next month, next year? It's about time somebody stood up to what's going on and said enough is enough. Are you coming with me or not?"

"Coming with you?" asked Stanley.

"Yes, coming with me to see Tyler and tell her what we think."

It was obvious that Stanley wasn't too keen on the idea. "Well, I need to get showered and then I could do with getting home after being out last night."

"So you're not coming with me, then?"

"I can't really, and I don't think it's a particularly—" Stanley's words were cut off in mid-sentence by Chloe.

"Fine, I'll go on my own then." She stormed off without looking back at him. He called after her, but she refused to acknowledge him.

Billy arrived at his shoulder, his shirt, hair and face thick with soil and grass. "What have you said to upset her?" he asked.

Stanley was about to take his frustration out on Billy when Mr Webster's shouting intervened. "Come on, you lads, get it sorted. Bathurst, get in there and get in that shower. Look at the state of you, lad, you're covered in mud."

Stanley and Billy made their way quickly towards the sanctuary of the changing rooms.

Chapter Thirty-Four

CHLOE WAS STILL angry even after she had got showered and changed. She grabbed her bag and headed straight over to the school offices, determined to see Miss Tyler and tell her exactly what she thought about the recent events at the school. She reported firstly to Mrs Tanner, the school secretary.

"Shouldn't you be going home at this time of day, Chloe?" she asked.

"I need to see Miss Tyler as soon as I can, please," Chloe replied.

"Well, we're very busy this evening due to the events going on in school. We've got the wedding fair, and we've also got local dignitaries and businessmen coming in for a little celebration in the hall with Mr Greenstock."

Chloe faked a smile as she was reminded of how things at school were taking a turn for the worse.

Miss Tanner was interrupted by the phone on her desk bleeping into life. "Look you'll have to grab a seat outside Miss Tyler's office and be patient, Chloe."

She picked up the phone and waved Chloe over to the grey seats outside the head's office. Miss Tanner smiled and spoke politely into the phone. "Shigbeth Middle School, how can I be of service?"

Chloe walked over to the seats against the wall by Miss Tyler's office. The door to the office was ajar and she could just about look in and see Miss Tyler's legs swinging underneath the desk as she chatted into her phone. Outside the window, a catering van was pulling up, with a man leaping out and then proceeding to carry trays full of food and other supplies in through the main doors, presumably for the business meeting in the hall. Miss Tanner came out from behind her desk and rushed off down the corridor. Everything quietened down, and Chloe sat there, starting to rehearse how she was going to get her point of view across to the headmistress without getting into too much trouble. She would have felt a lot better if Stanley had been with her, but he obviously had more important things to do than help the cause. He'd joined the rest of the children at school – happy to sign a petition, but when it came to actually fighting for what they believed in they were nowhere to be seen. She would have to do this on her own.

The wait continued as Miss Tyler continued to talk on the phone. Chloe wondered if she even knew she was there waiting for her, and so crept over to the door and nudged it ever so slightly further open. Miss Tyler was facing away from the door. She was still on the phone, but was sat facing towards the far wall upon which various school photographs were aligned symmetrically. Carefully, Chloe moved closer until she was actually in the room. Hopefully, Miss Tyler would notice her, end the telephone conversation and Chloe would get the opportunity to do what she had come here to do. For a moment, she thought about coughing or knocking on the door to grab her attention, but for now she decided to wait silently until maybe Miss Tyler turned round and could see her first. Chloe waited and listened to what the head was saying, watching Miss Tyler play with her hair as she looked up at the photographs on the wall.

"Rest assured there will be nothing stopping you tonight. They arrived this morning and everything is as it was the last time. You come in, you fill the van, you go and no one will be any the wiser."

Chloe's pulse raced. She couldn't quite believe what she was hearing. Who was Miss Tyler talking to, and what a strange thing to be saying?

"Just remember, after this one, I'm done. I've come through on my part of the deal. You just make sure you come through on yours. Tonight it is."

Miss Tyler clicked off her phone, paused for a second in thought, and then straightened her outfit and hair before heading off down the corridor to the business presentation in the hall. Chloe had already gone.

Chapter Thirty-Five

SIDNEY HAD BEEN feeling pretty chipper and jolly today. His friends had turned up last night for their inaugural expedition as the Shigbeth Justice League, and both Terry and Bobby had expressed their enjoyment and determination to do it again. Although, it had been agreed that they should wait a couple of nights, and that it was something that they would do together once in a while, certainly not every evening. There was still a risk: with the three of them together now, they stood an increased chance of being seen and attracting the attention of the general public, the press and even the police. They had all agreed that this was something they desperately hoped to avoid, not to mention the potential for discovery by their own families, although Terry did point out that his cat Houdini wouldn't bat an eyelid if he caught him slipping out of the back door at one in the morning in his Skunk ensemble.

Coupled with the successful mission last night was the call that Sidney received mid-morning from the job centre. Unfortunately, they hadn't found a job for him just yet, but the nice lady on the other end of the phone did mention that she was waiting for a few new opportunities to come through in the next forty-eight hours from firms who might well be interested in employing drivers. That news boded well for Bobby too, who was looking for work in that particular field.

That sense of hope assisted Sidney in ignoring the abject weather outside and put a bit of a spring in his step. He would share the optimistic news with Stanley tonight after school, which would of course lessen the blow of the revelation about him losing his job in the first place; something which, he would be keen to point out to his son, wasn't his fault. He was just another hapless victim of the growing use of technology in the workplace and corporate imperialism; he'd heard all that on a documentary that he watched earlier in the day. He didn't really understand it, but it certainly sounded impressive and served as a useful explanation as to why he had been temporarily thrown onto the employment scrapheap. It would be a great weight off his mind, coming clean to Stanley. Sidney hated lying to his son and was finding that he was having to do this every day now. Stanley might sometimes look daft, but he wasn't. At some point he would figure out that his father's stories of stomach aches, back problems and going into work late, and the continued absence on the driveway of the delivery van, just didn't add up. Sidney's little secret about his nocturnal adventures as the Raven would remain undisclosed, of course. Today, he had even had a shave and clipped his toenails; things were looking up.

Meanwhile, Stanley trudged home in a much gloomier mood. He'd spent the morning being bored out of his wits doing business studies and the afternoon out in the rain for Mr Webster's PE lesson. To add to his misery, he'd had a bit of a falling-out with Chloe. Tiredness had been a factor in that; he had been up for half the night on their pointless stake-out, and now all he really wanted to do was get home, watch some telly, have some decent food and then go to bed and forget about today. It was nice, however, that when he did arrive home, his dad seemed to be up and about and in a cheery mood. He even made him a cup of tea. Something was clearly wrong. Stanley's sixth sense was proven right when his dad plonked his cup of tea down and sat at the kitchen table opposite him. He started clearing his throat for a big announcement.

"Stanley, I've got something that I need to tell you," he began with a serious, earnest look on his face. Blimey, he'd even had a shave, thought Stanley.

"I haven't been telling you the truth for the last week or so. I think it was Monday when I started, or was it Tuesday? I can't quite remember exactly when it was if I'm being honest and, well..." He paused as his brain searched to find the words of explanation that he needed. "What I'm trying to say is that you know all this stuff about me going into work late, and you remember I had a bad back as well? Was that on Tuesday or was that Wednesday? I've sort of forgotten now, but anyway. Oh, and you know the van hasn't been here for a few days; did I tell you it was in the garage, or was that connected to the exercise regime that I was telling you about – you know, that one with Terry Funk? It's all sort of connected to him in a way, because it's happened to him as well. Not just him actually; there are quite a few of us by all accounts, not that I have anything to do with them any more as I just couldn't face it, you see."

Stanley stared back at him. "Dad, just tell me what's going on, please."

Sidney looked his son straight in the eye and sat upright again in his chair. He took a deep breath. "Okay, cards on the table. Here we go, let the dog see the rabbit, eyes down for a full house, let's have a look at what you could have won, et cetera."

Stanley leant towards him, waiting for his dad's mouth to reach its final destination.

"Truth is, I've lost my—"

"Van?" interrupted Stanley.

"No, I've lost my—"

"You've lost your keys to the van?"

"No, not the keys to the van; I've lost—"

"The plot?" guessed Stanley.

Sidney fell back into his chair, exasperated. He was just about to speak again when there was a hard, repetitive banging at the door. "Who the flipping heck is that?" he exclaimed.

Stanley shot up out of his chair. "I don't know, but it sounds urgent, Dad. I'll have to get it."

"If it's one of those charity collectors, tell them they'll have to keep some of the money back for themselves to pay their medical bills because I'm going to find all the coins in the house and shove them—"

Fortunately, there was another huge rap at the door before Sidney could complete his sentence.

Stanley raced into the hallway, and such was the ferocity of the knocking that even Sidney rose from the kitchen table to take a gander at who it was making such a racket. Stanley opened the door to find a breathless Chloe on the front step. "What on earth's wrong, Chloe?" he asked, worried.

"We've got to talk, Stan," she said, squeezing the words out between puffs of breath.

Stanley looked back at his dad.

"Don't worry, son – you deal with Chloe and we'll finish our conversation in a minute," Sidney instructed. He retreated back into the kitchen. Stanley closed the front door and joined Chloe in the front garden.

"Are you okay, Chloe? What is it? Tyler hasn't expelled you, has she?"

Chloe was trying to settle herself down before explaining what she had come to say. "No… no, it's not anything like that. We need to go out again tonight, you, me and Billy."

Stanley was still confused. "Okay, but why?" he asked.

"They're coming tonight," said Chloe.

"Who's coming tonight?"

"The computer thieves. They're coming back for the new ones. I heard Miss Tyler talking to them on the phone in her office. She's involved in this too. It's all arranged, and we need to stop them, and we need to tell PC Green all about this."

Stanley tried his best to calm her down. "Okay, but let's just take this one step at a time, Chloe. How do you know for sure that Miss Tyler was talking about the computers?"

"I don't know, but it's just the way she said it – something about them having no problems again this time, putting things in a van and like it was some sort of deal that had been struck already. And it's definitely happening tonight, I heard her say that."

"Chloe, it could have been a call about anything. Miss Tyler could have been talking to her boyfriend or even a parent about something. It might be something perfectly innocent."

"It feels right, Stanley. I just know it. They're coming again tonight and she's part of it, I'm sure of it."

"But you've got to admit that you're getting too caught up in all that's going on at the moment, and you were already angry before you went along to see her this afternoon. Couldn't it be that you are putting two and two together and making five?" he challenged.

Chloe paused and flashed a look of hurt at Stanley. "So that's what you think. You think I'm making all this up, do you? I suppose you're going to let me down like you did this afternoon?"

"I didn't let you down this afternoon, Chloe."

"You didn't come with me to see Miss Tyler, though, did you?" she charged.

"No, I didn't but… look, I'm sorry if you feel that way, Chloe, I really am, but—"

"You're just like the rest of them at school. I thought you were different, Stanley Rain, but now I know better." Chloe looked at Stanley with indignation and disappointment. She turned away from him and moved off down the pathway, away from the house.

Stanley didn't know which way to turn. His dad was waiting for him in the kitchen. His best friend was walking away from him. He hesitated.

"Look, Chloe, wait up," he cried and bounded after her.

Chloe turned round to face him.

"Okay then, you win. I'll come with you tonight."

Chloe's face lit up with delight and relief. "Thanks, Stanley. We need to get organised, and we need to get PC Green."

"No PC Green, Chloe. We can't involve the police with something that we have no evidence for. Let's just take a camera and we can take photographs or call him on your phone if the thieves arrive. Let it just be us three to start with," Stanley insisted.

"But what if it's dangerous?" she asked.

"We'll be hidden like last time, and at a safe distance. If anyone shows up, we'll call the police and stay out of the way. Besides, Billy will be with us and he is trained in those sorts of things – well, according to him anyway. Let's go home and get some tea and then we'll meet at Billy's later – say, six o'clock – and talk it all through calmly." He placed his hand on her shoulder and looked her in the eye. "I promise I'll be there with you; like I should have been this afternoon."

Chloe smiled again and gave Stanley a bone-crunching hug. He went bright red.

Chapter Thirty-Six

"YOU MUST TAKE after me, son," remarked Sidney as Stanley returned to the kitchen. "I've had hundreds of women over the years banging the door down to get to me. I know exactly what it's like to be irresistible to women. I used to think it was my top aftershave, Shark Bait, that did it, but I eventually realised it was just me."

Stanley did sometimes consider whether his dad actually believed what he was saying and was simply deluded.

"What were you trying to tell me earlier, Dad?" he asked, eager to return to the real world and the unfinished business they had been discussing before the arrival of Chloe with her revelation from school.

"Sit down, Stanley, I've got something important to say."

His dad gestured for Stanley to return to his chair at the kitchen table. They sat down opposite each other and Sidney tried again. This time it was quick and easy.

"I've lost my job." Sidney looked really surprised that he had just thought it and it had popped out of his mouth straight away.

"Thank God for that," replied Stanley, dropping his shoulders, sinking back into his seat and breathing out like a balloon releasing air.

"What do you mean, thank God?" asked his dad.

"I'm just glad you're all right and it isn't something medical. When you were telling me before that you had so many problems, I started thinking about you being ill in bed and I feared the worst. And you're off your fry-ups and eating muesli instead like you've been ordered to by a doctor. It suddenly hit me that this was what it was all about."

Sidney shook his head. "No, you don't have to worry about my health. I'm as fit as a fiddle, me. I'm even thinking of signing up for the darts team at the Rose and Crown next season. The reason why the food menu here has gone downhill is because I've got to start watching my pennies now I've lost my job and there's no income coming in. That's why we're eating muesli for breakfast."

"So we're doing that to save money?" said Stanley.

"Well, we're certainly not doing it because it tastes nice, are we?" Sidney confirmed. "But, Stanley, it's important that you know that there are already firms interested in employing me. I've had my agent down at the job centre fighting off calls for me this week. Word's got out that I'm available. I think I'm being headhunted. I'll most probably have a better job by the start of next week. We'll be off muesli as soon as I can, I promise."

"That'll be great, Dad. I miss our morning fry-ups."

"Here, have a look in that cupboard behind you, Stanley; we might have a few chocolate biscuits left in there. I'll put another brew on and we'll treat ourselves."

"Did you hit someone?" asked Stanley.

"What?"

"Is that how you lost your job?"

"No, I most certainly did not hit anyone; not this time anyway." Sidney carried on talking as he got up to grab a bottle of milk out of the fridge. "It's not just delivery drivers like me. Even Terry Funk got made redundant and he worked in the office. A new firm has just taken over and we've all been replaced by technology. I heard about it on the news the other day; it's the next stage of evolution, where humans are replaced by computers."

Stanley was reaching for the cupboard doors above the washing machine to get to the rumoured chocolate biscuits. "The opposite's happening at our school. We had all our computers nicked this week, so at least the humans there are back in control."

The bottle of milk suddenly slipped from Sidney's grasp and smashed on the tiled floor.

"Blimey, Dad, are you okay?" asked Stanley.

His dad was stood with his mouth open like the entrance to a tunnel. He didn't seem interested in the broken glass or the milk that was now spreading all over the kitchen floor.

"Just do what you just did with those cupboard doors again, son." He motioned.

"What?"

"Just open the doors and close them again, will you?"

Stanley did as he was told. He pulled the two doors open like he had to get the biscuits, and pushed them shut afterwards. "Is everything all right, Dad? You've gone all weird." He was right. His dad suddenly seemed lost in thought. Eventually, he came out of his trance.

"Right, don't touch any of this mess; I'll clean it up later. I've got to speak to Terry," he said.

"When will you be back?"

"I won't be long; I've just remembered that I promised to meet him and help him with something. I'm going to be late if I don't get going right now. You'll have to sort your own tea out, mate, I'm afraid."

"But, Dad, there's not much in the house, and I'll have to stay out of the kitchen anyway because you've smashed the milk bottle," protested Stanley.

Sidney immediately fished in his pocket and pulled out a ten-pound note. He thrust it into Stanley's hands. "You'll have to get something from the chip shop again. I'll sort myself out later when I get back."

Stanley was amazed. It was a whole ten-pound note that he had been given, and for once his dad didn't seem to want any of it for himself and hadn't even mentioned getting any change. This was a historic moment in the Rain household. Stanley seized the opportunity to take advantage of his father's goodwill while he was frantically searching for his jacket and preoccupied with meeting up with Terry as soon as possible.

"I'm having a sleepover at Chloe's tonight, Dad. That's what she was excited about earlier. Billy's coming too. Is that okay?"

Sidney shouted back as he hurtled out of the back door, "No problem, son. Be good and I will see you tomorrow."

Stanley kissed the ten-pound note and gave a little fist pump of celebration. He now had the perfect excuse for the new stake-out tonight as well.

Chapter Thirty-Seven

SIDNEY COULDN'T MANAGE to run all the way to Terry's flat, but he gave it the best go he could. He would have hailed a taxi if he could, but he'd given the only money he had in his first pocket to Stanley for his tea. The bit of change in his other pocket would have only just managed to get him to the end of the street in a cab. As he huffed and puffed along the way, things started to come back to him about the events that preceded his fall from the wall a few nights ago. Previously, he knew that he had been at the school but for the life of him he couldn't recall why until just then it felt like a lightning bolt had hit him, back in the kitchen with Stanley. At the very same moment that his son was reporting that the computers had been stolen from school during the night that week, he had pushed the doors to the biscuit cupboard closed.

It was this that jolted Sid's memory, and he finally remembered what he had witnessed at the school that fateful evening. From his viewpoint on top of the garden wall, he saw the doors to the van pushed shut by two men. The lettering on the doors combined to form the word *Greenstock*. Furthermore, he recognised the two men closing the van doors as the assistants that had been with Nigel Greenstock when he was sacked. He was an eyewitness to an actual crime taking place, and he now knew the man that was responsible for it.

"We need proof, Sidney. I'm just as keen to see Nigel Greenstock get his comeuppance for this as you are, but you can't just go to the police without any evidence that a crime has been committed," Terry pointed out.

Sidney had nearly knocked Terry's front door clean off its hinges when he first arrived. It had taken a good few minutes and a cup of tea for him to calm down and carefully reveal his story step by step. Although it never crossed Terry's mind to disbelieve what his friend had revealed, Sidney's thoughts on what to do next did lack logic and common sense.

"How on earth do you expect the police to believe your story that you'd gone out for a walk to get some fresh air at God knows what time in the morning? Then you saw the crime and decided to climb a wall for a better view, but you fell off and bumped your head. This apparently caused you to forget what happened, and that explains why you haven't been to the police since to tell them. It doesn't make any sense, Sidney. They won't believe you. You need proof or evidence other than a story. We need to come up with a better plan of action than that."

"Such as what?" demanded a frustrated Sidney.

"I don't know yet. Give me a second to think," replied Terry, taking a moment to slurp from his cup and then scratch his semi-bald head. "We could go back to the school and look for clues there," he suggested, "or we could patrol the school tonight in case the villains come back?"

"Don't be stupid, Terry, these guys aren't idiots. They won't come back to the scene of the crime only a couple of days later."

"Okay then, why don't we go back to where we used to work?" suggested Terry.

"Just walk into the depot in broad daylight?" asked Sidney, a little perplexed.

"Not in broad daylight, but we go back tonight; as the Justice League, me, you and Bobby." Terry had come to life. He had a twinkle in his eyes. "We could find the evidence there and then go to the police."

"You mean go to Greenstock and break in? I don't really want to go to prison, thanks very much, Terence."

Terry stood up from his chair and wandered over to his sideboard. "Who said anything about breaking in?" He pulled open a drawer and pulled out a set of keys, jangling them in front of his spectacles. "They may have taken my stapler, but they forgot to ask me for my keys before I left."

Sidney's bottom lip fell away from his top lip like a drawbridge. "Terry Funk, you are a naughty boy." They both smiled and rewarded themselves with a little chuckle.

"I'd best get my Skunk outfit ready for this evening. There are criminals that need to be caught." Terry beamed.

"I'll get to Bobby's and see if the sergeant is available for a little mission," said Sidney. "We'll meet at the depot at one o'clock in the morning."

"You going to be able to sneak out tonight, then?" enquired Terry.

"Stanley's at a sleepover at his friend Chloe's. I've got the evening completely free, and I'm going out on the town."

Chapter Thirty-Eight

"I CAN'T; NOT tonight anyway. It was risky enough last night without doing it again straight away. I'm bound to be found out. You said we should only do it every so often for that very reason," complained Bobby.

There was a shout from upstairs. "Who is it, Bobby?"

Bobby winced and then called back towards the heavens. "Don't worry, dear, it's just Stanley's dad again, my little wallflower. He's looking for Stanley because his tea is ready."

"Tell him that Stanley's not here. He's gone with Billy because they are having a sleepover at some girl's house tonight. I can't remember her name," shouted Mrs Bathurst.

"It's Chloe," Sidney shouted up the stairs. There was a pause for a moment.

"No it isn't," came the reply, "Joey's a boy's name."

Bobby intervened in an attempt to explain. "No, love, it's Chloe. Sidney says she's called Chloe."

There was another pause as the two men awaited a response from Mrs Bathurst. They nodded at each other and gave a quick smile to fill the awkward silence.

"Bobby?" came another shout.

"Yes, petal?" he replied.

"Get rid of him," Mrs Bathurst demanded.

Sidney frowned and was about to say something back, when Bobby quickly ushered him out of the door and escorted him away from the house and down to the front gate.

"Sorry about the wife, Sidney, she's under a lot of pressure with me not working and she isn't very sociable at the moment. Look, tonight is going to be too much of a risk for me and I'm not sure I'm cut out for this sort of thing."

"We need you, Bobby. You're exactly cut out for this type of caper; your military experience might be needed. It'll be like the Special Forces working behind enemy lines. If we can get some evidence then we'll have solved a major crime here," argued Sidney. "I know we sometimes don't get on perfectly, but I think that's because we're both used to being leaders rather than followers. We are both used to giving orders rather than taking them, and sometimes it gets in the way of our partnership."

"What partnership?" asked Bobby.

"The Shigbeth Justice League, Bobby; the promises we made at the pub when we each took a piece of the beer mat, remember?"

"Sidney, I can't do it, mate. She'll kill me if I get caught going out at night messing about. And if I get into trouble with the police for breaking into somewhere then I'm in even deeper bother. Maybe next week or something, I don't know; I'll have to weigh things up and see how it goes."

Bobby opened the front gate and sighed. Sidney realised that nothing he could say was going to change his mind. Reluctantly, he strode through the gate and started back down the road, turning his head back to face Bobby as he left.

"You're not the man I thought you were, Bobby Bathurst," said Sidney.

Bobby didn't answer. He just closed the gate and went back to the house. Deep inside, he knew that Sidney was right. As he walked in through the front door, Mrs Bathurst was stood there waiting for him at the bottom of the stairs. She was wearing a fluffy white dressing gown and was busy filing her nails.

"You got rid of him, then?" she asked.

"Yes, dear, he's just left," answered Bobby.

"Good," she replied.

"There's no need to be quite so rude, darling. Sidney is a friend of mine."

Mrs Bathurst turned her nose up and a sour look washed across her face. "I suppose he's another loser who can't find a job?"

Bobby straightened his shoulders and responded

firmly. "Do you mean, is he currently unemployed and looking for work? Yes, he is actually."

Mrs Bathurst reared up on her feet to respond. "Well, I don't want him anywhere near my house again. We've got enough useless men in here without another one turning up."

"It's my house too, and I say he can come here whenever he wants."

"It's *my* house, Bobby Bathurst, not yours. I'm the one who pays the bills round here while you sit around all day and night watching telly when you should be out grafting like what I am," she screamed.

"Well, you can have your house, my love, if I'm not worthy enough to be in it. I'm going to get some of my stuff, and if you need me for anything I'll be in the games room at the back of the garage."

"You can stay there all night if you want. What makes you think I need you round here anyway?"

"Right, I'm going there right now," said Bobby.

"Right, go on then," said Mrs Bathurst.

"Right this minute," confirmed Bobby.

"Don't let me stop you," encouraged his wife.

"Right then," said Bobby, "I'll just get myself some clean pants for the morning." He stomped upstairs. Mrs Bathurst screwed her face up and carried on working on her fingernails.

Chapter Thirty-Nine

IT ONLY TOOK a few seconds for Billy to come on board and join Chloe and Stanley for the new stake-out that evening. When Chloe told him what she had heard outside Miss Tyler's office, he didn't stop to consider whether it might have been a perfectly innocent telephone conversation rather than part of a conspiracy to steal computers from the school. Stanley had a suspicion that they were embarking on another gigantic waste of time. If she was being honest, Chloe wasn't sure either but something in her gut said that she was right on this one and tonight the thieves were coming back to school to grab the computers that had only just arrived that very morning. Billy excitedly packed a holdall full of everything he needed including his torch, night-vision goggles and camera.

At least other things had fallen into place this evening. As far as their parents were concerned, they were all at each other's houses. Stanley and Billy were spending the night at Chloe's and Chloe was supposed to be at Stanley's. Miss Scott was okay with that as it suggested that there was a chance of her meeting Stanley's dad again at some point in the future, so any blossoming of her daughter's friendship with Stanley Rain was fine by her. Once she had found out that Chloe was away for the evening, she had straight away got on the phone to organise a girls' night out with her friends. This would allow the gang to hang out at Chloe's until dark before assuming their positions overlooking the school entrance as they had done the night before. Once finished with their stake-out, they would sneak back to Billy's 'office' before heading to school from there.

Everything seemed to be falling into place. Even the weather was much improved, with the showers of the afternoon giving way to clearer skies. Stanley seized the opportunity to tell Chloe about the revelation that his dad had lost his job, and that although he was concerned about it, he did feel strangely better that his dad had come clean with him and there was hope for a new and better job on the horizon. Considering the situation he was in, Stanley felt altogether calmer and happier than he had been the night before. As they waited in the dark outside the school gates, he borrowed Billy's binoculars to gaze in wonder at the stars.

He must have fallen asleep at some point. He'd occupied that midway point between being conscious of where he was and a world of dreams, peppered with characters from his everyday life such as his father and

Miss Tyler. Then he became aware of Chloe nudging him, trying to wake him up. Stanley's head rose up from the rucksack that he was using for a pillow. He wiped his mouth and eyes with his sleeve and tried to get a bearing on precisely where he was and what he was supposed to be doing.

"What time is it?" he asked.

"Never mind that," whispered Chloe, "we've got visitors."

Stanley's eyes readjusted to his surroundings, but it was the noise that first alerted his senses; a deep rumbling sound, which then all of a sudden stopped. Someone had turned an engine off. Somewhere, doors opened and shut with a metallic clunk. Chloe and Stanley froze in the dark and silently wondered what their next move was to be. Chloe gasped as a gentle clatter came from just above them. Billy lowered himself down from the apex of the tree to join them on the grass. His face was once again plastered with camouflage paint.

"It's a truck," he said, stating the obvious.

"What's it doing here at this time of the morning?" asked Chloe.

"Maybe it's a delivery or something?" said Stanley. "Then again, I suppose it's a strange time to be delivering stuff, when the school is shut and there's nobody around to take it in."

"I think we should call the police," suggested Chloe. She took Constable Green's card out of her jacket pocket.

"But we can't be certain what's going on yet. Let's wait a bit longer and just be sure," counselled Stanley.

"I think Stanley's right, Chloe. We probably need to hang on a bit and check that there's definitely a crime taking place. I can't get a good enough view from up the tree even with my night-vision goggles on. We need to get closer," advised Billy. "I'll go. I've done this sort of thing before."

"Are you sure, Billy?" checked Chloe.

"Yeah, we do this sort of stuff all the time at the agency."

"No, I mean are you sure you are okay taking a closer look?"

"Yeah, don't worry. They won't even know I'm there. I'll take my camera, though, and take some photos. Don't ring the police till I come back," Billy instructed. Then he checked he had his camera with him and handed his night-vision goggles to Stanley. "They're not working very well tonight anyway."

"Probably because they're just a pair of toy binoculars with some red plastic on the lenses," said Stanley.

"Do you need my walkie-talkies?" asked Billy.

"Best if we keep radio silence for this mission," noted Stanley.

Billy gave a nod and then a thumbs up. "Back in a minute," he said. Then he sprang away towards the school entrance clutching his camera, and melted into the darkness.

Chapter Forty

BILLY CREPT CLOSER and closer to the heart of the action. Sure enough, a large van had pulled up to the back of the canteen at the side entrance to the school. A couple of lights had been switched on in the school and a set of doors had been opened. Billy crouched by a fence and then decided to run down into the school site between an outbuilding and a set of classrooms. He darted behind the metal bins that were housed at the side of the canteen and held his position for a moment. This would hopefully give him a really good view of what was unfolding.

He heard footsteps scraping the concrete between the open doors to the school and those at the back of the van. Someone was walking back and forth between the two, but the doors and the lack of light were blocking his sight of who it was and what exactly they were up to. He knew it was a risk and his heart was pounding, but he needed to get closer if he was to capture any photographic evidence of theft. Billy readied himself and waited for the footsteps to disappear; then in the gap that presented itself before they returned, he vaulted over the bins and ran over to the side of the van, crouching in the shadows by one of the front wheels. He was now so close that he could hear somebody else breathing as they stopped at the doors and then skidded whatever was being carried along the floor of the van.

The plan that Billy came up with was a dangerous one. The next time the man returned to the van, he would jump out and grab a quick photo. Whether he was seen or not, the rest of his plan was quite simple: he would run for his life back to the others.

Chloe and Stanley had also nudged themselves closer to the suspicious goings-on within the school premises. They couldn't really see anything from their former position among the trees, and neither of them much fancied climbing a tree to get an aerial perspective of what was happening or heading into a danger zone that might see them come face-to-face with hardened criminals. Instead, they opted to move towards the edge of the fencing, where they hoped they would be just far enough out of the picture to avoid being seen, but near enough to make out what was going on. From here at least they had a pretty decent view of the side of the van and could see the shadowy outline of someone marching back and forth between the two sets of doors. It was clear to them that they were bringing items, possibly boxes, from the school and then depositing them in the back of their transport.

"They are thieving things," whispered Chloe. "It must be the computers. I was right about what I heard, and Miss Tyler's involved in this too, I knew it!"

Stanley caught a glimpse of a small figure running across from the bins over to the front wheel of the van. "There's Billy," he said, nudging Chloe so that she could locate him.

"Blimey! He's a bit close for my liking, Stan. He's going to get caught."

"There's definitely a robbery going on. Get the phone ready, Chloe; I think it's time you gave Charlie Green a call. We'll ring 999 too afterwards; the more police here, the better."

Chloe reached in her pocket for her phone and was just about to make the call when Stanley grabbed her arm. "What's he doing?" he whispered in alarm.

Chloe looked across at the van and saw the outline of Billy moving towards the back of the van, while the thief disappeared from view back into the school. Both Chloe and Stanley held their breath, transfixed at what was materialising.

Billy timed his move to the back of the van to perfection. He was ready and waiting behind the back door as planned. As he readied his camera to get the evidence he needed, he noticed the word *Green* in large letters across the door in front of him. He made a mental note of that and then took a deep breath. A man was coming out from the school. Billy peered around the side of the door to have a look. He had overalls on, and a cap pointed downwards which hid his face from view. In his arms was a cardboard box. *Chloe was right*, Billy thought. *They must be the new computers that only arrived this morning.* Maybe it was the very same guy who'd stolen Billy 2000 Junior and the original Billy 2000? With that realisation, Billy gritted his teeth and looked to make his move. He would wait for the man to get closer to the back of the vehicle, and then he would quickly nudge his head around the door, take the photo and disguise himself in the shadows behind the door once again. If he moved fast, he calculated that there was a very good chance that he wouldn't be seen.

Billy bravely went for it; his head poked into view for a fraction of a second and he clicked the button on the camera. It was only when the immediate vicinity was flooded in light that Billy remembered about the flash.

The guy in the overalls approaching the van dropped the package he was carrying when the camera flash went off right in front of his face. The cardboard box thudded onto the floor and the man's head jerked back in shock. Billy just stood there, frozen in time as his brain quickly tried to engage and recalculate the new situation that had developed. His first reaction was to hesitate as to which direction he should run in. He set off back where he had come from, but the man in the overalls had stumbled back over that way and was busy trying to come to terms with what was happening. Instead, Billy moved across the open back of the van, unable to take his eyes off the figure in front of him.

Because of this, he didn't know that there was another figure that had been in the back of the van, collecting and stacking the items as they arrived. The first he knew about this other person was when he felt a hand grip his holdall, preventing him from any urgent getaway.

"Come here, you," his assailant shouted, spinning Billy round as he held on to the shoulder strap of his holdall. There was a brief struggle as the bag fell to the floor, but Billy could not free himself entirely from the powerful grip of whoever was behind him.

The one dressed in overalls had recovered from the blinding flash of the camera and began yelling, "It's a blinking kid. What's he doing here?"

Billy was now in a bear hug with strong arms locked around his chest. He kicked his legs up into the air in an attempt to wriggle free. He tried to shout for help, but his voice was then muffled by a heavy hand clenched across his mouth. Then he was turned around before being bundled into the back of the van to land amongst the cardboard boxes. Before he could find his bearings, the outside world was closed off from view as the doors were slammed shut. He was trapped.

Outside the van, the man in the overalls quickly found what remained of the smashed camera on the floor and scooped it up. "What do we do now?"

"Let's get out of here," the other responded, jerking a set of keys out of a pocket.

"What about the kid?"

"Let's worry about him later. Ring the boss man and tell him the score," he instructed. "Come on, quick."

Chloe and Stanley held their breath. They saw Billy dart out from behind the door. Then there was a sudden flash of light, and for a split second everything near the van was lit up. There was some sort of commotion and then shouting, a couple of bangs as doors were closed and two men ran around to the front and clambered into their seats. The engine roared into life and the wheels squealed into motion. The van sped away from the school and headed out of the gates before hurtling around the corner and onto the main road. Chloe was on the phone as they ran across to look for Billy. The school doors were still open and the lights on inside illuminated a solitary cardboard box lying on the concrete. Billy's holdall was there too.

"Billy? Billy? Where are you?" shouted Stanley feverishly. His eyes searched everywhere for a sign of his comrade.

Chloe looked petrified as she explained to PC Green where she was and what she'd seen. She looked at Stanley for news of Billy, but all he could do in response was stare back and shrug his shoulders.

"Oh my God," she said into the phone. "They've got Billy. He's been kidnapped."

Chapter Forty-One

THE RAVEN SCANNED the industrial estate. Nothing moved, and the dark of night shrouded the area in an eerie black blanket. Every so often a street lamp pitched a circle of orange light onto the pavement and road. The gaps in between provided the welcoming areas of invisibility that the Raven flitted in and out of as he stealthily moved towards the depot where he and Terry used to work before that fateful day when Nigel Greenstock took over the firm and starting firing people from their jobs. Sidney's gloves traced the edge of the wall across to the main doors. His black cloak wrapped around his body and he momentarily disappeared from view. He crouched in a bush and listened intently for sounds that would signal the arrival of his partner. Sidney pressed a button on his watch, which confirmed that it was fast approaching one o'clock in the morning, the arranged meeting time of what was left of the recently formed Shigbeth Justice League.

Right on cue, another figure came running across the car park. His cape, with its thick white stripe running down the centre, flapped in the breeze he created as he ran. A familiar face, partly disguised by a black cycle helmet and a pair of swimming goggles strapped around his forehead, arrived next to the Raven and knelt down. Skunk reached into a pocket in his cargo trousers and a silver set of keys emerged, glinting in what little light there was.

"Are you sure about this, Sidney?" he asked.

"We need evidence, Terry. Let's do this," Sid replied.

"Do you think we ought to do the Justice League chant before we start?"

Sidney shook his head. "It won't be the same without Bobby," he determined. "Let's leave it till later."

The two allies hauled themselves to their feet and approached the main doors. Skunk used a small torch from one of the many pockets in his trousers to illuminate the keyhole, while the Raven scoured the horizon for unwanted observers. Terry smiled as the door opened with a satisfying click, and before they stopped to think again about what they were doing, they were inside the building. Terry locked the door behind them, strode over to a box on the wall and started pressing buttons. Sidney could hear a faint beeping noise in the background.

"It's got an alarm! I didn't realise," whispered Sidney.

Terry finished pressing the buttons and the bleeping stopped. "Good job I know the code for it, then, isn't it?" he said with a look of pride on his face.

Sidney exhaled and relaxed. "Right then, Skunk, my old friend. Let's find those computers or anything else that proves that Greenstock was behind the theft at the school."

They bounded off together up the stairs towards the main office where Terry used to work. When they arrived, they quickly shut the blinds on the windows and switched on a few desk lamps so that they could see a little better. Sidney took his mask off and Terry pulled his goggles down from over his eyes.

"Well, they might not have changed the alarm code but there have certainly been a lot of other changes around here," remarked Sidney.

The two stood there amazed at the transformation that had taken place in the days since they had been sacked. New desks were in place, with shiny new keyboards, computers and monitors on all but a few of them.

"Bingo. We've found lots of computers," said Sidney.

"Yeah, but how do we prove that these are from the school, if indeed they are the ones stolen from the school in the first place?"

"Look, Terry, I saw a Greenstock van being loaded with stuff from the school and Stanley said that lots of computers were taken the other night. There's got to be something around here that links this firm to that theft. The question is, where exactly?"

Terry looked around and contemplated where their evidence might be. "Okay, you start looking at these computers; I'll try Greenstock's office." They split up and started searching.

Five minutes later, Terry came out of Nigel Greenstock's office clutching something in his hand.

"What is it, Terry, you found something?"

"Not really," admitted Terry; "no evidence, anyway. But I did find this rather nice stapler." He placed it on a desk underneath a lamp so they could both see it and appreciate it.

"Very nice," said Sidney.

Terry pressed it a couple of times and seemed impressed. "Yes, it's got a lovely smooth action, hasn't it? It grips nice too. Have a try for yourself, Sid."

Sidney fired off a couple of staples into a wad of paper. "It's a little cracker, Terry, make no mistake about it."

"Of course, it won't replace the one that Nasty Nigel Greenstock stole off me, but it is a beauty, Sidney, there's no denying that."

"Take it," urged Sidney. "No one will notice that it's missing, and he took yours, didn't he? What does it say in the Bible; an eye for a tooth and a tooth for an eye?"

Terry certainly was thinking about Sidney's idea, but decided against it. "No, that would be stealing and

I would be doing just as he did in taking my stapler off me. We must stick to our morals here, Sidney. We're a force for good after all."

Suddenly, there was a noise from down in the car park. Terry and Sidney urgently replaced their mask and goggles and flicked out the desk lights that they had put on. They crept over to the windows and carefully lifted a blind to check out what was going on outside.

"Looks like we are in deep trouble, Sid," concluded Terry.

Down below in the car park, a van had pulled up next to one of the loading bays at the side of the depot. The doors were open and two figures in overalls with caps on their heads seemed to be arguing and pointing at each other.

"What do we do now?" asked Terry.

"I don't know. But I do know that our situation is getting worse by the second. Look who else is here." Sidney's finger traced along a fold in the blind to point at a new vehicle arriving at the depot; its headlights streaking across the car park. The black sports car pulled up adjacent to the van and someone got out.

"It's Greenstock!" said Terry in alarm. "We're done for."

Sidney hesitated and gathered his thoughts. "But they don't know we're here, do they? And anyway, what are they doing here at this time of night?"

"So what's our next move?" asked Terry.

"Stay here and keep a watch over things. I'm heading down the back stairs to the loading bay for a closer view. If all hell breaks loose, get away down through the front entrance and call the cavalry."

Sidney released his hold on the blind and puffed out his chest. "And so it begins," he announced dramatically.

"What begins?" queried Terry.

"I don't know," replied Sidney, "I've just always wanted to say that. I think it's in a movie or something." Then he was gone.

Chapter Forty-Two

THE RAVEN STEADILY made his way down the back stairs in the darkness, feeling his way along the banister with gloved hands and ensuring that the soles of his boots connected carefully with the steps. Along the way he could hear the odd voice some way off, and there was definitely movement from somewhere in the building. He dodged inside the area where vans would come to load up with packages for delivery throughout the parish. Sidney knew every nook and cranny of this area and it wasn't an issue for him to find his way over to the van in spite of the lack of light. The van seemed identical to the one that he had seen a few nights ago when he had his heavy fall and suffered the temporary loss of his memory. He sneaked up to the back of it; the doors had been closed, the name *Greenstock* emblazoned across them. The area was empty. There was no sign of either Nigel Greenstock himself or his hired hands. Sidney took a deep breath and pulled open the doors to take a look at what was inside.

There, amongst a load of stacked cardboard boxes, he was shocked to see somebody rolling around on the floor making muffled noises of distress. Suddenly, it didn't matter whether he was caught or not as his immediate priority now was helping this apparent prisoner. Sidney hauled himself into the van and pulled his head torch on across the top of his mask. He flicked it on to find a child of about twelve years old peering up at him with scared eyes. Silver tape had been wrapped around his ankles, wrists and mouth in order to keep him there and keep him quiet. A moment after the light from the head torch had illuminated the scene, there was a look of recognition in the eyes of both prisoner and rescuer. The tape was removed from the young boy's lips.

"It's you. It's the Raven!" cried Billy.

Sidney was working as fast as he could to free the tape from around the boy's legs. He had recognised him, but kept his mouth shut and refused to acknowledge that this was Billy Bathurst, son of Bobby and friend of Stanley. What he was doing stuck in the back of the van he didn't know, but there would be time for questions and answers later.

"I knew you were real. I should have known that you would come and rescue me," Billy cried excitedly. "They've been stealing computers from the school and I tried to stop them, but they grabbed me and shut me in this van. On the way here they stopped for a moment and put all this tape around me because I was shouting and banging on the doors."

The Raven placed a gloved finger to the mouth of his mask, prompting the young boy to be silent for fear that their escape attempt would be discovered. Perhaps it would have been wiser, he thought, to remove the tape from the boy's arms and legs first before allowing him to talk and potentially draw attention to themselves? He worked frantically, using a small knife from his pocket to cut away the rest of the tape. Eventually, Billy was free.

"Thanks, Mr Raven; any chance of an autograph or a signed photo?"

Sidney gripped Billy by the shoulders and whispered, "Listen to me. We haven't got much time and I need you to promise me that you will do exactly as I tell you."

Billy nodded; eager to please and wary once again of the serious predicament that he found himself in.

"You must run away from here back to the main road. Knock on a door with a light on, hail a cab or a passing motorist. Get help and get the police." He helped Billy to his feet and down from the van to the ground. The two nodded their goodbyes and then Billy ran out of the depot and away.

Sidney quickly scanned the area and then headed back into the bowels of the vehicle to see what was in the cardboard boxes. He grabbed his pocket knife again and ran it across the top of one of them before pulling apart the lid to look inside.

"Bingo," he muttered. "The computers from the school, just as Billy said."

Then something crashed down over his back and he fell on top of the box. Sidney rolled around on the floor of the van, trying to catch his breath. Someone or something had landed a blow on the top of his back with a sickening thud. He screwed his eyes open and exhaled in an attempt to absorb the pain and get himself up off his feet just as soon as his body was physically able to do it. Above him, shining in the glare of his head torch was a tall figure in overalls with a cap on. Sidney searched the floor desperately for something to protect himself with.

"You looking for this?" the figure mocked. "You should keep your beak out of other people's business." The tall figure had Sidney's pocket knife in his right hand, and held it up in the air.

Sidney gulped as the man stepped towards him. Then he noticed another figure appear at the man's shoulder; another man in overalls with a cap on his head. Maybe the blow he had taken had brought on double vision?

Suddenly, a cardboard box appeared in the air above the two men before it came crashing down on the head of the first. The man with the knife collapsed in a heap at Sidney's feet, the weapon spinning out of his hand and landing on the floor of the van with a metallic rattle. Then the second figure was reaching down for Sidney's hand and hauling him to his feet. Sidney began to realise that this stranger had probably just saved his life.

"You were right, my friend. You did need me after all," the man said.

"Bobby?"

"Sergeant Squirrel to you, brother," he replied. "I think that's what they call downloading," nodding at the man crumpled on the floor of the van underneath one of the computer boxes.

Sidney winced as he straightened his back and steadied his weight back on his two feet. Bobby Bathurst wrapped an arm around him for support.

"Glad you could join us, Sergeant." Sidney smiled. "Better late than never."

Chapter Forty-Three

SKUNK DUCKED DOWN behind a desk as he heard footsteps at the top of the stairs and the doors were thrust open. Somebody walked across the room, around the desks and computer terminals, before disappearing into Nigel Greenstock's office. A light was switched on inside – perhaps it was Greenstock himself, Terry thought? He hesitated. He'd been told to keep watch over the van and the car park below, but now he couldn't do that in case he was seen by the man in the office. He had also been told to leave by the front stairs and entrance if there was trouble, but he hadn't seen anything untoward go on and he didn't know where Sidney was either. Instead, he opted for crawling along between the desks and running down the stairs leading down to the loading area. That was where Sidney had gone and the man in the office had recently emerged from. Terry pedalled his arms and legs across the floor as quickly as he could. Halfway across the room he stopped and took a quick glance into Greenstock's office. Someone was in there talking on the phone. It was him; it was the boss, Nigel Greenstock. Terry recognised the slicked-back hairstyle, and though he wasn't wearing a suit like he usually did, he still managed to look smart even in more casual attire. Terry didn't hang about staring for long. He kept low and fast and soon he was away down the stairs in search of Sidney.

On his way down, Terry saw a light coming from one of the storerooms by the toilets on the first floor. Carefully, he moved closer to the entrance, hugging the wall so he was out of view. Somebody was in the storeroom moving boxes around between the shelves; Terry could see the back of him at the far end of the room, dressed in overalls and with a cap covering the back of his head. Terry edged closer. The keys were still hanging in the door and he noticed the light switch on the wall. A plan formulated rapidly in his head. Silently, but as quickly as he could, Terry reached into one of the many pockets in his cargo trousers and clutched a number of capsules within. He took a deep breath. The man inside was still busy pushing the boxes around the storeroom. Terry's gloved hand crept up the wall to the light switch and turned it off, plunging the storeroom into pitch black. Then he drew back his arm and hurled several of the stink-bomb capsules as hard as he could down onto the floor. His left hand pulled the door shut and his right hand turned the key in the lock. Terry placed the keys in one of his pockets and waited. There was a commotion from inside and someone started pounding on the locked door. A strange, sickly smell started to emanate from the room, and eventually the noise and banging stopped. Skunk smiled and turned round, placing his hand over his nose as the smell drifted through the air along the corridor.

"Oh dear, I hope I've not killed him," he thought out loud. "Perhaps I should just use the one in future?"

Just then, a shaft of light appeared from down the stairs to the ground floor below, becoming a large circle as it got closer and closer. Terry reached into his pocket in search of more ammunition as what looked like two figures got closer. One of them had some sort of bird mask on and a cloak.

"Sidney, is that you?"

"That's it, tell everyone my real name why don't you, Terry?" he replied.

"Hi, Terry – I mean Skunk," greeted the other man, smeared in face paint and wearing brown.

"Bobby – well, I mean Sergeant Squirrel! Where on earth did you come from?"

"There's not time for that," said Sidney. "We've just taken one of them out downstairs and found a vanload of computers from the school, I reckon."

"What's that smell?" coughed Bobby, pressing a hand to his face in disgust.

"One of them is locked in there. I used the Skunk crystals on him. I think he might be dead."

"We will be in a minute if we don't get out of here," warned Bobby.

"Greenstock's upstairs in his office," revealed Terry.

Sidney had the back of his hand up to his mask for protection against the smell of the stink bombs leaking out from the storeroom. "Right, you two get back downstairs and grab a couple of those computers from the van for evidence. I'm going after Greenstock."

"Are you sure, Sid? Shouldn't we all go after him?" suggested Bobby.

"You get the computers; I'll deal with him. This is personal," Sidney explained, and tore off up the stairs to Greenstock's office.

Chapter Forty-Four

NIGEL GREENSTOCK STOPPED talking into his phone for a moment when the man dressed in black, with the cloak and the belt and the boots and the bird mask, strode into his office.

"I've got to go," he said, "something's come up."

Greenstock looked concerned. He left his chair and walked out from behind his desk. He stood at the side of it, checking for potential escape routes and wondering where his two assistants had gone.

"Who are you?" he asked.

"I'm your worst nightmare," the figure replied. "I'm the Raven."

Greenstock flicked a strange sort of smile which somehow oozed both confidence and nervousness at the same time.

"You've been a very naughty boy, haven't you?" accused the masked man.

"What do you mean?"

"All those computers that you have in there and in the back of the van are stolen, aren't they?"

Greenstock laughed. "I'll think you'll find that they are more sort of… borrowed. I own the school now. Didn't you know?"

There was no reply from the Raven, who stood menacingly in the middle of the room.

"That was my lawyer on the phone. He'll be along in a minute. Reckons I've got nothing to worry about. Says that it's all explainable and above board. You see, Mr Raven, or whatever your name really is, you don't seem to realise that you've chosen to tackle a very powerful man." Nigel Greenstock suddenly confidently walked out to stand at the front of his huge desk, right in the eyeline of his new adversary. "You see, I've got a few things that people like you will never have, such as talent, intelligence and above all money. I'm a very, very successful businessman and I'm used to taking what I want when I want it. Anyone or anything that gets in my way can be dealt with just like that." He clicked his fingers and a nasty, cocky grin broke across his face. "You see, you wouldn't know because you don't have any of those things. I can buy schools, hospitals, people, whatever takes my fancy, and no one can stop me. I'm a bit like a God really, when you come to think about it. You can't hurt me. You can't do anything to me. I'm untouchable." Greenstock nodded his head in self-congratulation, propped himself on the front of his desk and made himself comfortable.

The Raven clenched his gloved fists and bit his lip beneath his mask.

"You won't find me needing to wear a mask in a pathetic attempt to hide my failures, my inadequacies and my weaknesses. I don't really have any of those." Greenstock stroked his fingers through his hair before continuing. "Clearly you do, dressed up in a costume like you're heading off to some sort of party for freaks. It's all very, very sad. I can't imagine what sort of desperate, lonely life you really live when you're not out at night pretending to be someone else. Do you need the mask because it makes you feel better inside? Less of a failure, perhaps?"

"Oh, I don't *need* a mask," whispered the Raven. He reached up with his hands and moved it away from his face.

"Do I know you?" asked Greenstock, trying to figure out where he'd seen that face before.

Then the Raven's fist hit him firmly in the face with huge force. Nigel Greenstock was propelled backwards over his desk to land in a heap behind it. His chair squeaked as it spun round after breaking his fall.

Sidney Rain sniffed the air. "Nothing personal, just business," he remarked. The Raven popped his mask back down, left a knocked out Nigel Greenstock on the floor behind his desk and went to find the others.

"What did you do with Greenstock?" asked Terry when Sidney reached the loading bay.

"We had a discussion about things. I disagreed with him, so I punched him in the chops."

"Fair enough," agreed Terry.

Bobby appeared from around the corner and placed the box he was carrying onto the floor. "We've got to get out of here, guys. We've got company. It's the police."

Terry turned to Sidney. "What do we do now?"

"Well, I'd love to stay here, have a chat and explain everything to them, but I can't. Let's get out of here."

The three friends pitched themselves out of the loading area with capes flapping behind them as the darkness filled with blobs of blue light from a police car.

Chapter Forty-Five

CONSTABLE CHARLIE GREEN screeched his police car to a halt and turned to the young boy sat on the back seat. "Stay in the car, Billy; this could be dangerous." The young policeman leapt from the vehicle and broke into a sprint towards the depot where the lights were on and a van was parked with boxes littering the floor. As he rounded the side of the van, he met three strange, costumed figures coming the other way. All four stopped and stared.

"Police, who are you?" he cried.

The man with the bird mask and cape stepped forward. "We're the good guys, Officer. We're on your side. We're leaving this to you."

PC Green was confused as he nervously faced up to the three men. He recognised that he was outnumbered and that this could get very nasty, very quickly.

"What do you mean?" he asked.

"There's a van full of stolen computers and more upstairs," said the masked man.

"There's a bad guy shut in the back of the van," added the man dressed from head to toe in brown. "He's got a bit of a headache. A box fell on his head."

"And another locked in a storeroom," said the one with white stripes everywhere, a bicycle helmet on his head and what looked like swimming goggles on his face. "I'd give it five minutes before you go in, though, if I were you. Hopefully he's still alive."

"The boss is upstairs in his office. He's had a tough day and is having a lie down behind his desk," said the leader of the trio. "You didn't see us, okay? You take the credit for all of this. No one can know who we are. Do you understand, Officer? If people know we exist then it will have massive consequences for Shigbeth. We must remain secret."

"Okay, I think I get it. But who are you guys?" queried PC Green.

"I'm the Raven," said Sidney, hands on hips.

"I'm Skunk," shouted Terry.

"And I'm Sergeant Squirrel," called Bobby, placing his hand up at the side of his back-to-front cap and saluting as if still in the army.

The three men came together and placed their hands on top of each other.

"Together we are the Shigbeth..." yelled the Raven.

"Justice..." cried Skunk.

"League," added Sergeant Squirrel.

"Ranger Force Shotgun!" added Skunk, and the

three sprinted off across the car park and away into the night.

Charlie Green stood there. "I don't think anyone would believe me if I told them," he said.

Chapter Forty-Six

WITHIN TEN MINUTES there were blue lights everywhere as other police cars arrived. In one of them were Stanley and Chloe.

"Blimey, this is the place where my dad used to work," shouted Stanley as they pulled up in front of the depot.

As soon as Billy saw them he forgot what he had been told by PC Green about staying in the police car and he ran out to meet his friends. Both Stanley and Chloe felt very happy to see Billy. Chloe ran over to him and gave him a tremendous hug. Stanley settled for a manly pat on the back and a handshake.

Soon, there was a parade of criminals as three men were led out of the premises bound in handcuffs. They were busy arguing.

"I got jumped in the van. There were undercover coppers everywhere," said the first.

"Tell me about it," moaned the second man, who Billy recognised from back at the school. "I got locked in a cupboard and they used some sort of gas on me."

He coughed and was straight away taken to be looked at by a first-aider.

The third one in the line was the main man himself, Nigel Greenstock, looking not quite as slick, stylish and confident as usual. His nose was covered in blood and it had leaked all down the front of his shirt.

"Someone grassed on us, boss. They knew we were coming," said the first man.

Nigel Greenstock didn't answer. He walked along forlornly with a shocked, glazed expression all over his face.

As the three were encouraged into the back of a waiting police van, a few of the officers came over to Charlie Green and started shaking his hand and patting him on the back. Then the young constable walked over to talk to the kids.

"Thanks for your help, you guys," he said. "What you did was very brave and extremely dangerous, especially you, Billy."

"Will they go to prison?" Billy asked.

"Well, we have plenty of evidence with the computers here. Certainly, Mr Greenstock and his cohorts are in big trouble. I can't imagine many will want to do business with him again after what he's been up to here."

"This might even end his interest in the school," Chloe pointed out excitedly. "Perhaps you ought to have a word with Miss Tyler too? I'm pretty sure she was in on this."

"Thanks, Chloe, we have officers going round to speak to her now after what you told them."

"And you know what the best part is? I got rescued by the Raven. He is the one that came into the van and cut me free," revealed a very animated Billy.

"I think it's been a very long night, young man." PC Green frowned.

"Honestly, he did. I saw him with my own eyes."

Chloe and Stanley giggled at each other and shook their heads in disbelief.

"Course he did, Billy," said Stanley in a patronising tone.

"Let's get you all home to your parents," said PC Green.

"I'm not making it up this time, guys. It was the Raven, honestly. He had this mask and a cloak, and he spoke to me."

Constable Green reached his arm around Billy's shoulder and started to accompany the three children back to his police car before taking them home.

Chapter Forty-Seven

STANLEY WAS THE last one to be dropped off at home. Both Miss Scott and Mrs Bathurst looked scared and angry when they answered the door to PC Green returning their children in the early hours of the morning. Stanley was very worried about how his dad would react. It took a good few raps at the door before his dad opened up, wearing his blue stripy pyjamas and looking the worse for wear. Stanley was ordered straight to bed, while his dad chatted downstairs with PC Green. After a while, the front door shut, the police car rumbled off into the night and Stanley could hear his dad marching up the stairs and across the landing to Stanley's bedroom. The door opened, and he walked across to Stanley's bed and sat on the end.

"Are you cross with me, Dad?" whispered Stanley.

"No, I'm not cross with you, Stan. But I don't want this happening ever again. Do you understand?"

"Yes, Dad, don't worry, it won't."

"Anything could have happened to you. I mean, that Billy Bathurst got kidnapped, by all accounts. You could have got hurt."

Stanley kept quiet, wondering how this was going to end and what punishment he might face for lying about being at Chloe's and being out during the night in such dangerous circumstances.

"Having said that, PC Green was insistent that you had been very brave and your thoughts were about helping the police and your community to solve a serious crime. That makes me a very proud dad, Stanley Rain, which is something I have always been since the day you were born." Sidney bent down and kissed his son on the cheek. "I know I should have told you earlier about losing my job. If I promise not to keep secrets from you in future, will you promise that you'll never lie to me again?"

"I promise, Dad. There will be no lies and no secrets."

"In that case, there's something that I probably need to tell you as well."

"What is it, Dad?" wondered Stanley.

"Well, you know Terry Funk and Billy's dad, Bobby? We've been getting together recently and we get on really well, like a team, and we've been planning something – a bit of a venture, I suppose you would call it."

"Yes, Dad?"

"Well, we're going to set up our own business. Terry is going to run the office and Bobby and I are going to do all the driving and deliveries and such. It's really exciting and we're going to go down to the bank on Monday to make all the arrangements."

"That's wonderful, Dad," cried Stanley, freeing himself from the bedcovers, grabbing his dad by the neck and giving him a terrific hug.

Sidney squeezed him back.

"We tell each other everything now, Dad. Like a partnership again," said Stanley.

"Yes, Stanley," replied Sidney. "No more lies, no more secrets."

When Stanley woke up later that morning, his dad had been down the shops already. They had an enormous fried breakfast, just like old times. Not a spoonful of muesli anywhere to be seen.

Chapter Forty-Eight

"THERE A FEW important final things that I want to share with all the students, parents and guests that we have here today, at this last assembly before we break up for the summer holidays," said Mrs Jeeraz.

Stanley, Chloe and Billy were sat together in the middle of the assembled students in the hall, extremely excited at the prospect of the school holidays that were about to commence. Among the parents sat at the back of the hall, there was slightly less excitement at the thought of their offspring spending the next several weeks at home rather than at school. Both Sidney Rain and Bobby Bathurst were there, stood at the back of the audience, having left Terry Funk back at the office in charge of their fledgling delivery business, which had been up and running for a few days now. Chloe's mum, Stephanie Scott, had also taken up to the invitation to come along to the final assembly of the academic year. Every so often she flicked a glance over her shoulder to check that Sidney was still there. She would hunt him down later.

Mrs Jeeraz continued from her prominent position on the stage. "Firstly, I need to tell you what a personal honour it is for me to have been chosen to lead Shigbeth Middle School, if only in a temporary capacity, for the new term in September, owing to the resignation of Miss Tyler. I can assure you that I intend to follow the great traditions of this school that has educated thousands of children in Shigbeth over the decades. Both myself and my new deputy, Mr Webster, will work tirelessly on your behalf." Mr Webster fiddled with his tie; it had obviously been a long time since he had worn one. He clutched his asthma inhaler in his hand in case of emergency.

"I should also like to remind you that the planned conversion of Shigbeth School into an academy will now not take place as scheduled due to the recent arrest of the proposed sponsor, Mr Nigel Greenstock, the managing director of Greenstock Clothing…"

At this point Sidney opened and closed his right fist to check whether the bruises on his knuckles had disappeared.

"…and that any future plans for this school will only be implemented after full consultation with parents and, most importantly, the students."

At this point, Chloe's smile lit up the hall.

"After all," Mrs Jeeraz continued, "it is our students who consistently show what incredible members of our local community they are. Three particular examples are with us today, and to finish off proceedings I would like to hand over to another stalwart of Shigbeth, Detective Charlie Green, the brave police officer who arrested Nigel Greenstock and his assistants virtually single-handedly."

As everyone in the hall clapped and cheered. The newly promoted Detective Green rose to his feet and walked across the stage to address the crowd.

"Good afternoon, ladies and gentlemen. My thanks to the new headmistress Mrs Jeeraz, and to you all for that lovely welcome you have just given me; I don't deserve it."

At this point, Sidney and Bobby turned to each other and nodded their agreement with what had just been said.

"What I am here to do today is acknowledge three very special students at this school who showed bravery, determination and community spirit beyond the call of duty when they helped to solve the mystery of who was stealing computers from this very school. Those stolen computers are back here today, being used by all the students, and I think that everyone in Shigbeth should recognise their remarkable achievements. As a small token of our thanks, each of them will receive a brand-new iPad. Therefore, I would very much like for Chloe Scott, Billy Bathurst and Stanley Rain to come up on stage now and receive our thanks and their well-deserved rewards."

The three friends rose from their seats and were enveloped in a sea of smiling faces, thunderous applause and whoops of support from all sections of the hall. As they made their way onto the stage to receive their gifts and shake hands with the new detective and headmistress, everyone in the hall rose to their feet and the photographer from the *Shigbeth Gazette* pitched forward to take a few shots for the evening edition of the local paper. Chloe and her mum grinned at each other. Bobby Bathurst almost saluted Billy, until Sidney noticed just in time and slapped him on the wrist to stop him. Stanley Rain's gaze met his dad's, and a look into his eyes revealed that there was no prouder parent in the whole of Shigbeth.

Chapter Forty-Nine

HE COULDN'T HAVE been more than fifteen years old. The hoodie around his shoulders and head kept his face and identity secret from the world. His pulse raced in his neck and his fingers fumbled in his pockets as he waited for the opportunity to present itself. Every so often he would take a quick, furtive glance towards the old lady behind the counter, who was busy sorting out items in boxes, ready for putting out on the shelves. In a flash, the hooded youth grabbed several chocolate bars from one of the shelves and stuffed them into the pockets of his hoodie. Before the lady could react, he was already pulling open the door and fleeing the shop into the darkness beyond, mission accomplished. With a big grin on his face and his arms wrapped around the stolen items in his hoodie, he bounded down the street away from the scene of the crime.

Suddenly, he became aware that he was not alone. Someone else was present, watching him carefully from the other side of the street. The young boy stopped and listened to the pulse of his heartbeat throbbing in his ears.

"Who's there?" he enquired of the figure half hidden in the darkness.

"What are you doing, naughty boy?" commanded a booming voice in response.

"Who's… who is… it?" said the boy.

A man stepped out into the street light. First came the boots, then the flap of a cloak, the gloves on his hands and finally a mask of some description.

"I recognise you now, Mister," the boy chirped. "You're that guy who chased me the other week. You're Fatman." His body folded up in laughter. "I don't believe it. You come back for more, tubby? You couldn't keep up with me last time; what makes you think you can catch me this time?"

Another figure stepped out from the shadows to the right of the masked crusader. He was dressed in black and white stripes, with what looked like swimming goggles on, and some sort of headgear. Then a second man materialised to his left, all dressed in brown with a sandy-coloured cape on his back, a cap on back to front and his face all covered in paint.

"Say hello to my little friends," said Sidney Rain.

"I'm Skunk," shouted Terry Funk.

"Sergeant Squirrel reporting for duty," announced Bobby Bathurst, saluting.

The three joined together and placed their hands on top of each other.

"Together we are the Shigbeth…" hailed the Raven.

"Justice…" cried Skunk.

"League," added Sergeant Squirrel.

"Ice Station Zebra!" yelled Skunk at the top of his voice, and the three sprinted off after the thief, avoiding treading on the chocolate bars scattered on the road as they went.

Chapter Fifty

CHARLIE GREEN'S PHONE went off at one o'clock in the morning. He reached an arm over to his bedside table and hurriedly answered it.

"Hello," he said.

"Police Constable Green?" asked a deep voice.

"Yes?"

"There's a delivery for you on your front lawn." The line went dead.

Charlie hastily wrapped himself in his dressing gown and snapped back the curtains of his bedroom window, but he couldn't see anything in the darkness. He ran downstairs and opened the front door. Sure enough, there in the middle of his lawn, wrapped in some sort of tape, was a boy of about fifteen years old. There were chocolate bars strewn all about him.

Just then, PC Green caught sight of someone watching him from over the road, away to his far left. Three men were there illuminated under a streetlight. They stood with hands on hips. One of them saluted. Charlie blinked for a fraction of a second in recognition and disbelief. When his eyes opened again, they had gone. Almost, as if they had never really existed and had simply been a figment of his imagination.